THE UNICORN CHRONICLES: BOOK TWO

SONG
OF THE
WANDERER

BRUCE COVILLE

SCHOLASTIC PRESS ◆ NEW YORK

Library of Congress Cataloging-in-Publication Data
Coville, Bruce.
Song of the wanderer / by Bruce Coville.
p. cm. — (The Unicorn Chronicles; bk. 2)
Sequel to: Into the land of the unicorns
Summary: Having jumped into Luster, the land of unicorns, Cara makes a perilous journey to bring back her grandmother, the Wanderer, in order to release the Queen of the unicorns and allow her to die.

ISBN 0-590-45953-8

[1. Unicorns — (Fiction. 2. Fantasy.]
I. Title. II. Series: Coville, Bruce. Unicorn Chronicles; bk. 2.
PZ7.C8344So 1999 [Fic] — dc21 98-40760

10 9 8 7 6 5 4 3 2 1   9/9 0/0 1 2 3 4

Printed in the U.S.A. 37
First edition, November 1999
Book design by David Caplan

Dedicated to all the readers who have waited,
patiently and impatiently, for this second volume,
with my deepest apologies for taking so long.

CONTENTS

CHAPTER ONE

A MEETING
WITH THE QUEEN

T he Queen will see you now, human child."
Cara scrambled to her feet. She had been sitting beneath a large quilpum tree, enjoying the spicy
smell of its bark while she watched the unicorns graze
in the blue-green meadow ahead of her. The afternoon
was warm, and she had been drifting at the edge of
sleep. Now she was totally alert.

Laughing Stream, the unicorn who had spoken to
her, watched with an amused expression as the girl began brushing leaves and twigs from her pant legs.

I wish I had some better clothes, Cara thought anxiously. *I'm hardly dressed to visit a queen!*

Indeed, she had been wearing the same jeans and
T-shirt since she had first entered Luster a few weeks

1

ago, and they were filthy. She put a hand to her long red hair and sighed. It was even worse than her clothes.

"Ready?" asked Laughing Stream.

Cara nodded. "Ready."

"Then follow me."

Though Laughing Stream was trying to be serious — this was important business, after all — the unicorn was not able to hide the hint of amusement in her voice. Cara would have been offended, except it hadn't taken her long after meeting Laughing Stream to realize that the unicorn found almost *everything* amusing. Her name had been well given.

Besides, the girl had no energy to spare on being offended. Her thoughts were all on what would happen when she saw the Queen. It was a conversation she had been eagerly awaiting since she'd arrived at Summerhaven three days earlier.

She had already seen the Queen a few times, but always in a very formal way. Today, at last, they were going to discuss how Cara would return to Earth to fetch Ivy Morris, the woman the unicorns knew as "The Wanderer," but whom Cara thought of only as Gramma.

The last time Cara had seen her grandmother, she was ringing the bell in the tower of St. Christopher's church to help open the gateway to Luster — the gateway through which Cara had fled with the amulet she now wore around her neck. From that moment, Cara had ached to know if her grandmother was safe, if she had survived that horrible night.

So intent was Cara on her thoughts that she paid no attention to where she was walking and soon stumbled over a root. She managed to keep from crashing to the ground, but just barely. Laughing Stream snorted, then tried to hide her amusement. Unicorns rarely stumbled.

They came to a circle of trees that reminded her of weeping willows, save that their trunks and leaves both had a distinct bluish tone. Their long, slender branches swept the ground, creating a kind of lacy wall. Laughing Stream led the way through an arched opening in that wall.

In the center of the trees shimmered a pool of crystal-clear water. A scattering of leaves, silver-blue and shaped like the blades of spears, floated on its surface. Standing at the edge of the pool was Arabella Skydancer, the Queen of the unicorns, sometimes known as "the Old One." She was small, her shoulders no higher than Cara's. Her mane was like the foam on the crest of the long ninth wave, her spiral horn like a lance of pearl. She held herself with a sense of ancient dignity that Cara found almost overpowering.

The Queen nodded to Cara and stared at her for a long moment. Finally, in a voice like soft summer wind, she said, "It is time for us to talk."

Cara lowered her head and made a kind of curtsy. Only a few days earlier she would have had to be touching the Queen in order to understand her. But now that the dragon Firethroat had given her the gift of tongues, she could speak with ease to any of the intelligent creatures of Luster.

The Queen laughed. A kind laugh, sweet and gentle. "No need to be so formal with me, child. Come, sit beside me. We will speak of what needs to be done . . . and of things you need to know."

Folding her slender legs, the Queen settled to a bed of young ferns. She was very old, but her age showed only in the way she was beginning to fade. Sometimes you could see right through her, as if she were already part ghost. Yet now, lying on the ferns, she looked as much like a young foal as an ancient queen. Except for her eyes. They were so deep and so old that looking into them made it hard to imagine anything had ever been young.

Cara settled beside her.

"Have you recovered from your adventures?" asked the Queen.

Cara thought before she answered. Her journey through Luster had been harrowing. But here at Summerhaven, safe and well fed, her body had quickly regained its full strength. As for her heart . . . well, that was a different matter. It was only days ago that she had discovered that the man who had chased her and Grandmother Morris into St. Christopher's had been her own father. She still stung from the knowledge that he was a Hunter, one of the ancient clan sworn to stalk and kill the unicorns. Even worse, through her father she herself was descended directly from the strange woman known as Beloved, the greatest enemy the unicorns had ever known.

She didn't know how to discuss these things with the Queen. They were painful and embarrassing. And frightening. Given her family history on her father's side, it sometimes surprised her that the Queen and the other unicorns would talk to her at all.

Yet her grandmother had been a great friend of the unicorns — such a good friend, according to her father, that she had stolen Cara away, kidnapped her, rather than let her fall into the hands of the Hunters.

But if that was so, why had her grandmother never spoken of it? Why hadn't she prepared her for all this? Cara loved her grandmother and longed to see her safe. But she also had some hard questions to ask her.

"I'm not sure I'll ever recover," whispered Cara.

"Each wound has its own time for healing," replied the Queen. "The wounds of the heart are much deeper than those of the flesh."

Cara nodded gravely.

"Now, let me speak to you of Luster," said the Queen. "If you are going to journey across our world in order to fetch the Wanderer, there are things you should understand."

Cara looked at her in surprise. "I thought I would use the amulet to return home." As she spoke her hand crept to her throat, and the chain that held the amulet her grandmother had given her — the amulet that had opened the way for her leap into Luster.

"Certainly the amulet will carry you between Luster and Earth," said the Queen softly. "But unless you make the crossing from the right place, you could still end up very far from your grandmother."

Cara felt suddenly weary. "Does that mean I have to go all the way back to where I was when I first got here?"

"Alas, if only it were that simple. But ours is an oddly patchwork world, Cara. We touch old Earth in a hodgepodge of places, connections that change with the passing of the seasons. That's why the first stage of your journey will be to the home of the Geomancer."

"The Geomancer?"

"She's a kind of . . . oh, an earth-magician. Her magic is that of soil and stone, of water and rock. She will be able to work out the best place for you to cross back to your own world."

"Is it far to where she lives?" asked Cara nervously. This was turning out to be more complicated than she had expected.

"Only two or three days. And you won't be traveling alone. We will choose a small glory of unicorns to travel with you. Only three, alas. I thought long and hard about this, whether it would be better to send a large group and seek safety in numbers, or a small group and hope for safety in stealth. I finally decided that a small glory would be wisest. After all, the delvers are already aware of you, and a large group would be more apt to attract their attention."

Cara shuddered at the mention of the delvers. The vicious, goblin-like creatures were sworn enemies of the unicorns. Her fear of them was intensified by the fact that one had attacked her shortly after she'd first arrived in Luster.

"I've asked Moonheart to lead the group," continued the Queen.

"That's nice," said Cara, despite the fact that the idea made her a little nervous. Moonheart was one of the Queen's nephews, and though he had been kind enough in the few days since she had met him, she found him distant and aloof. She suspected this might be partly because the very first unicorn she had met in Luster — and the one to whom she had really given her heart — was his own nephew, Lightfoot. For some reason Cara had not been able to discover, Moonheart considered the young unicorn a disgrace to the family.

Whatever the reason, Lightfoot and his big, lumbering friend the Dimblethum had quietly slipped away from their group just before they'd arrived at Summerhaven. Cara missed them both desperately. They had been her first friends in Luster; had helped her, taught her, and guided her on her journey to find the Queen.

Well, at least Thomas the Tinker and the Squijum were still with her. She would see them later, after her audience with the Queen.

Suddenly Cara realized that she had let her attention wander — an old problem that had gotten her in plenty of trouble in school.

"I know Moonheart may seem a little . . . formal," the Queen was saying. "But he is experienced in the ways of the forest and the mountain, and as brave as any unicorn you can find in all of Luster."

"It will be an honor to travel with him," said Cara quickly, feeling she had been terribly ungrateful to question the Queen's choice. *You're getting spoiled!* she told herself. *Not long ago, the idea of even seeing a unicorn would have been enough to make you think that your greatest dream had come true. Now you're getting choosy about which ones you want to travel with!*

"You will need him, and the others," said the Queen. "Luster is beautiful, but it is not without its dangers. Remember, our world is not developed in the ways that your world is. You will not find wide roads and solid bridges to cross this wild country. And along the way you may find strange and ancient creatures, beings that you thought no more than myths or legends."

Cara grinned. "You mean, like unicorns?"

The Queen laughed — a sound that made Cara think of distant wind chimes. "Like unicorns. But not only unicorns, child. We were the ones who opened the way, with the help of an old magician named Bellenmore. But once the gates were opened, others came through as well. As you know, we have dragons here. Dragons, and other creatures, too — some of them kindly, others more . . . unpredictable."

"Tell me more about the gates," said Cara.

The Queen paused for a moment, as if the subject was painful. "Seven gates link Luster to Earth," she said at last. "Stepping through any of them will carry you from one world to the other. I have kept them open in the hope that the day might come when we could finally return to Earth, or at least visit our old home more freely. Alas, I fear it was a fool's hope."

When Cara started to object the Queen shook her head. "Oh, yes, child. Even a queen can be a fool — perhaps more a fool than most. Many in my court feel it is time to close the gates, and not merely for safety's sake. They want to bring full end to our old connection. My heart speaks against this. But the truth is the choice may be beyond me anyway."

"Why?"

The Queen looked away, almost as if she were gazing into another world. "The ancient magic that formed the gates seems to be fading. It is possible they will vanish of their own accord sometime in the near future." She shook her head. "That will be a loss for both worlds. Anyway, for now — and for as long as the gates are open — each entrance to Luster is closely guarded at all times. And their location on Earth is a very deep secret, as it must be to keep the Hunters from passing through."

Cara felt herself blush at the mention of the Hunters from whom she was descended.

The Queen, as if sensing her discomfort, said softly, "I care much less about your roots than about how you have chosen to grow, child. You have well demonstrated both your loyalty and your courage. I am satisfied."

11

Cara felt a hot lump of sorrow in her chest when she thought of the moment in Firethroat's cave when she had been forced to choose between her father and the unicorns. *But he had been going to open a new gate, so he could lead the Hunters into Luster where they would kill —*

She cut off the thought. She had made her choice: She stood with the unicorns.

Yet the memory of her meeting with her father raised another question, almost as painful: *Where was her mother?*

According to her father, she was waiting to see Cara again. The thought pierced her with longing. But was it true?

Again she had let her attention wander. With a start, she realized the Queen was speaking.

"Tonight we will have a ceremony at which you will pledge yourself to the quest. Tomorrow, your journey will begin."

Arabella Skydancer paused, and Cara could sense a deep sorrow in her. "May that journey be successful. An old wound separates your grandmother and myself, and I would like to heal it. Bring the Wanderer back to me, Cara. Bring her back, because I dare not finish fading until you do."

"Finish?" asked Cara nervously.

"I am old," said the Queen, and the sudden weariness in her voice seemed to crush Cara's bones. "Older than I should be. I yearn to leave this life behind and move on to what is next. But I have promises to keep, and wounds to heal, and I cannot go until I do. So bring your grandmother back, child, for her sake . . . and for mine, so I can rest at last."

Cara felt a coldness in her heart. "Are you saying that if I bring my grandmother back —"

She couldn't bring herself to finish the sentence. The thought was too horrible. But she didn't really need to ask the question. Arabella Skydancer had made her meaning clear: She was waiting for the Wanderer to return so that she could die.

CHAPTER TWO

"Do You Accept This Task?"

Night fell. The moon, waning since the night Cara had confronted her father in Firethroat's cave, was a mere sliver now. The greatest light came from a huge star that the unicorns called "The Magician's Eye."

When the star reached its highest point, the unicorns gathered, arranging themselves in a half circle so that all of them were facing a large black stone. The stone, which had a perfectly flat top, was about three feet high, three feet wide, and five feet long.

When the gathering was complete Arabella Skydancer appeared, climbing silently onto the stone platform by way of its sloping rear side. She stationed herself at its center. Her milky white coat seemed to glow in the moonlight. She gazed out on the gathering, then called Cara to come and stand before her.

The girl stepped forward. Surrounded by the glory of unicorns, she felt unexpected tears well up. To be in this place, with these enchanted creatures, was a dream come true. But now she had to leave. Never mind that the leaving was to fetch her grandmother, something she desperately wanted to do. It still hurt.

She brushed a strand of her red hair away from her face, then reminded herself not to fidget and dropped her hand back to her side.

Arabella Skydancer, the Queen, the Old One, stared down at the girl for a long moment. Finally she said, "Cara Diana Hunter, do you accept this task of your own free will?"

"I accept this task of my own free will," replied Cara, using the ancient words of ceremony that the Queen had taught her that afternoon. "I will give it all my heart, all my strength, all my energy."

"So be it," said the Queen. Raising her head, she said, "I call Moonheart to come forward and join us."

A large unicorn stepped into the circle and came to stand beside Cara. He was so tall that he and the Queen were eye to eye, even though she was standing on the black rock. His horn was a pearly wonder: Extending a full three feet from his forehead, it glowed as if with some inner light — though Cara knew that he could quickly quench that glow if he needed to move unseen through the night.

The Queen spoke softly. "Moonheart, I ask you to accompany this child as she goes to seek the Wanderer. Do you accept this task of your own free will?"

Moonheart lowered his horn until its tip touched the stone between the Queen's cloven hooves. "Ivy Morris was a friend of mine," he said solemnly, "and our fates are tangled together like the strands of a callum vine. I accept this task with joy. I will give it all my heart, all my strength, all my energy."

Cara looked at Moonheart in astonishment. How was his fate woven with that of her grandmother?

"There will be danger," warned the Queen.

"I understand that."

"You may even be required to return to Earth."

A shudder rippled along Moonheart's silken flanks. But all he said was, "I will do what I must."

"Then guard the child," said the Queen. "Guide her

as well. Have you spoken to those we selected to travel with you?"

"I have," replied Moonheart. Turning toward the assembled unicorns, he made a series of low whickers, which Cara understood to be a call.

Two unicorns stepped from the group. One, a male, was the biggest unicorn Cara had yet seen. Coming from the other side of the group was a female who, though much smaller than the male, had such a look of ferocity that Cara found her almost terrifying.

"Greetings, Finder," said the Queen, addressing the big unicorn.

"Greetings, My Queen," he replied softly, in a voice that reminded Cara of a cello.

"And Belle," said the Queen, turning to the female. "Though I shall miss having you as part of my guard, it pleases me that you will be part of this journey."

Belle nodded, but said nothing until the Queen repeated the ceremonial words. Then she made her pledge and affirmed that she accepted the task of her own free will, just as each of the others had.

When the swearing in was finished, the Queen stepped down from the rock. Coming to each of them, she placed her horn across their shoulders in sign of blessing. "I shall eagerly await your return. May your journey be successful, for each of you is dear to my heart — as is the Wanderer you go to seek."

She returned to the stone platform. "Travel safe, travel well," she called, her voice stronger than Cara would have thought possible from such a seemingly frail creature. "May those who have gone before be always with you."

From behind them, in response, came the voices of the assembled glory. "Travel safe, travel well. May those who have gone before be always with you."

The Queen turned and left the circle.

The other unicorns waited until she was out of sight, then began to drift away as well. Several came over to bid a special farewell to one or the other of the unicorns going on the journey. But finally it was just Cara standing with the three who were to accompany her. She was longing to ask Moonheart about his connection with her grandmother, but before she could get up the courage, he said, "We leave at first light. I suggest you all get a good night's rest."

Then he, too, turned and left the clearing.

Cara felt uneasy as she watched him disappear into

the forest. Though it would be a great honor to travel with him, she found herself longing for Lightfoot. The younger unicorn was not only much friendlier, he actually seemed to like her — a feeling she did not sense from Moonheart.

She wondered if one reason she and Lightfoot got along so well was because they were both young.

Well, "young" isn't exactly the right word, thought Cara with a smile. Her friend was more than a century old, after all. But, according to what he had told her, that was approximately what being a teenager was to a human.

What she had not been able to get Lightfoot to tell her was why he had refused to return to the court at Summerhaven. No one here had been willing to speak of it, either — though in the few days Cara had been here, it had become clear to her that the unicorns at court were as unhappy with Lightfoot as Lightfoot was with them.

Her wandering thoughts were called back to the present by Finder, who said shyly, "I'm glad we'll be going with you."

"For all the use you'll be," muttered Belle.

"Fighting isn't the only way to be of help," said Finder gently.

Belle snorted, then turned to go.

"Wait!" said Cara.

Belle turned back.

"Thank you for agreeing to come."

"Moonheart asked," replied Belle sharply. "Of course I agreed."

"Belle is very fierce," said Finder, sounding a little nervous.

"Have to be fierce if you're on delver patrol," snapped Belle, her voice dripping with scorn. "Only way to survive."

"You can always hide," replied Finder. Then, quickly, he turned away. Cara had a feeling that if he were human he would have been blushing.

"I will see you in the morning," said Belle brusquely. Then she turned once more and left the clearing.

"Don't mind her," said Finder after Belle was gone. "She doesn't like to talk much."

"I guess not," said Cara, who could not help but wonder if her own family history had anything to do with Belle's attitude.

"I, too, will see you in the morning," said Finder gently. He nuzzled the top of her head once, then turned and disappeared into the darkness.

◆ ◆ ◆

Cara remained in the center of the clearing for some time. Though it seemed that the unicorns had all gone, she knew they would not leave her entirely alone; one or two were always somewhere nearby to guard her. She understood this was to protect her from delvers, but sometimes she suspected, sadly, that this was also to protect *themselves* from *her*. Despite all she had done, she was not sure the unicorns entirely trusted her. Given her family background, she could understand that. But it still hurt, especially considering what she had given up to be here among them.

Her thoughts were interrupted by the snapping of a twig. Turning quickly, she saw a man step from the darkness beneath one of the trees. The brief instant of panic faded when she realized it was Thomas the Tinker. As always, her friend was dressed in an outlandish coat, the original material of which had nearly vanished beneath a myriad of brightly colored patches. The coat had almost as many pockets as patches, and gold watch chains hung in graceful arcs from every one of them. A stray shaft of moonlight piercing through the forest canopy reflected off the chains, and also off the shiny scalp of Thomas's balding head.

"I didn't know you were here," she said as he crossed to join her.

"Wouldn't have missed a ceremony like that," he said, speaking as rapidly as usual. "I understand you're leaving first thing tomorrow?"

"That's the plan. Moonheart isn't the type to wait around once something has been decided on."

"Unicorns are like that." Thomas took one of his watches from a pocket, opened it, glanced at it, shook it, closed it, then placed it in a different pocket. He returned his attention to Cara. "I'd be glad to travel with you for at least part of the way, if you like."

Cara's delighted response was interrupted by a triumphant cry of "Hotcha gotcha!" as a furry ball of energy came flying out of a tree to land on her shoulder.

She jumped in surprise, then sighed as she realized it was only the Squijum. The creature raced down Cara's side and began to scamper in circles around her feet. "Want to come!" he chattered. "Want to come along!"

Cara knelt to bring herself close to him. Just over a foot high, he looked like some odd cross of squirrel and monkey. His thick fur grew in two shades of gray — light on his face, limbs, and stomach, storm-cloud dark on his head and back.

"It could be dangerous," she said earnestly.

The Squijum's enormous eyes grew even bigger, the bright blue pupils flashing. "No scared! No scared!" His bushy tail thrashed back and forth. "Good fight! Good run! Hotch hittem bad things! Bite bite bite! Want to come!"

"I doubt you could stop him if you tried," said Thomas, who was rummaging in one of his numerous pockets. After a moment he produced a hard biscuit, which he tossed to the Squijum.

The creature caught the tidbit with one three-fingered hand and scampered back up the tree, where he began munching on it. "No stop!" he confirmed between bites. "No stop Squijum!"

"Suit yourself," said Cara, secretly glad to have him along. Though she sometimes pretended that he annoyed her, she found his unreserved affection comforting.

The Squijum followed her to her resting place after she told Thomas good night. Buildings were not allowed in Summerhaven. Even so, she had a private spot to call her own — an open circle, about eight feet in diameter, surrounded by a wall of shrubs that grew so thickly it was impossible to see through them. In one spot the shrubs overlapped for about four feet; an opening about a yard wide between the overlap formed a kind of hallway through which Cara could enter. She wasn't sure, but she had a feeling that some human friend of the unicorns had caused the bushes to grow this way. Or maybe the unicorns themselves had done it, using their magic to create a comfortable resting place for their guests.

Within the circle she had a bed of moss and leaves, which she covered with a finely woven cloth Thomas had given her. Most nights the air was so sweet and warm that Cara was perfectly comfortable sleeping outside. It had rained only once since her arrival at Summerhaven; on that night she had slept in Thomas's wagon.

The Squijum entered the circle with her. Once inside, he went bounding around the green walls, now disappearing among the leaves, now bouncing out again to cry, "Hotcha gotcha!"

Cara settled herself on her bed, then stared into the star-spattered sky. She wondered — as she did several times a day — where her grandmother was, what she was doing.

Though the other questions — whether her grandmother was a captive of the Hunters, or whether she was even alive — were too awful to consider, they sometimes managed to creep in at the edges of her mind. Usually she was able to push them away.

Usually, but not always.

She stared at the stars above her, so many more than she ever saw in the light-choked sky of the cities where she had grown up. The *many* cities. She wondered now if all the moving she and her grandmother had done had been because they were fleeing the Hunters.

Or had it simply been because her grandmother was a Wanderer and could not stay in one place?

A falling star caught her attention. She began trying to pick out the patterns of the stars. Though different from the ones she knew at home, they were gradually becoming familiar to her.

She located the constellation Thomas had taught her to call "The Ravager." As she studied it, other questions came crowding in on her. The Queen had said it would take two or three days' travel to reach the Geomancer. But how long beyond that would it take to reach her grandmother? Would the journey really be as danger-ous as the Queen seemed to think? And, the biggest question of all: Would her grandmother even be there when she finally made it home?

Of course she'll be there, she told herself angrily, trying to ignore the fearful voice inside that kept insisting the Hunters would have come and taken her grandmother by now. *It wasn't Gramma they were after,* she reasoned, trying to make the fear subside. *It was the amulet. That was why my father followed me through the opening into Luster. Besides, he was alone. There was no one else there to bother Gramma.*

Though she kept repeating this idea, she could never entirely convince herself it was true.

Another frightening possibility occurred to her: What if Gramma Morris had already gone somewhere else to live, in order to throw the Hunters off the trail?

She tried to push the idea away, telling herself it was stupid. But her mind would not let go of it. She knew her grandmother would do whatever was necessary to shield the unicorns. The thought of making the long journey home, only to discover her grandmother was gone, had fled somewhere else, tormented her — partly because her heart was already tender on this matter, still unhealed from the loss of her parents. Which led her wandering thoughts back to the horrible question her father had planted in her mind, the question that had nagged at her ever since: Had her grandmother really stolen her from her parents in order to keep her away from Beloved?

And if she had, was that so bad? But why hadn't she said anything?

The questions blurred together. The Squijum, who had crept onto her bed and nestled in beside her, had fallen asleep. He was making a sound somewhere between a purr and a snore. The night air whispered around them, rich with scents of earth mold and moonflower.

She was still gazing at the Ravager when her eyes grew too heavy to keep open, and she fell asleep.

Her first dream was simple and sweet.

It was the second dream that made her wake up screaming.

CHAPTER THREE

THE JOURNEY
BEGINS

The dream had started simply enough. Cara was in the rented house she had shared with her grandmother for the last year or so, sitting in her own room. Feeling lonely, she went to look for her grandmother. But Ivy Morris wasn't there — not in the kitchen, nor the little living room, nor her own snug bedroom.

Finally, to ease her loneliness, Cara turned to their old black-and-white television, which her grandmother had insisted stay off most of the time.

To her surprise, it was already on.

And the picture was in color.

When Cara realized what was on the screen, she tried to turn away. To her horror, she couldn't; her eyes were locked on the image it presented.

This was how Cara saw for the first time the face of Beloved, the ancient enemy of the unicorns and her own many-times great-grandmother. Beloved, who as a child had watched her own father — a man who had been led by a lie to believe unicorns were evil — fight to the death with Whiteling, the unicorn who had come to cure her when she was horribly ill. Beloved, who still carried in her heart the tip of Whiteling's horn, which had broken off when her father attacked the unicorn and had forever after been both constantly wounding and constantly healing her. Beloved, who blamed Whiteling for her father's death (and her own never-ending pain) and, as a result, had vowed to destroy all unicorns.

The woman was shockingly beautiful, her face neither young nor old. Though her hair had turned pure white, it was still as thick and glossy as a unicorn's mane. Her eyes were gray, the deep gray of thunderclouds, save for their center, where they glowed a fiery red.

"You belong to me," the image whispered.

"I don't!" Cara cried. "I *don't!*"

"You're mine, Cara Diana Hunter, and always will be!" The scarlet pupils of Beloved's eyes were blazing now, so large and bright they almost obliterated the gray surrounding them. Her voice dropped to a whisper, low and seductive. "There is no point in fighting me, child. Blood calls to blood. And you *are* of my blood, my many-times great-granddaughter. So come to me. *Come to me!*"

"No!" cried Cara. She screamed — a real scream, so loud that she woke herself. She sat up, staring into the darkness, then gasped in new horror as she realized she hadn't been dreaming after all. Even though she was now awake, she could still sense Beloved in her mind.

"Get out!" cried Cara. "Get out!" Frantically, she shook her head from side to side, as if she could somehow fling Beloved away. "Get out, get out, *get out!*"

Beloved didn't go. "Accept your destiny, child of my children's children," she crooned in Cara's mind. "Accept who you are. No need to wander in vain. Come home — home to *me.*"

Trembling with horror, Cara beat at her head, trying to drive out the intruding presence.

"Come to me," whispered Beloved one last time, her voice desperate, longing.

And then, suddenly, she was gone.

Cara lay panting on the grass, scarcely aware of the Squijum crouched at her side, muttering nervously, "Hotcha Wowie bad dream! No good, much yell yowie yowie yowie."

Seconds later, Thomas and Moonheart came running into her clearing, both kneeling beside her to ask what had happened, if she was all right.

She flung her arms around Thomas's neck and clung to him, weeping.

Later, after she had grown calmer, Cara told them what she had experienced. At the first mention of Beloved's name, she could see a hint of fear in Moonheart's eyes, a flicker of distrust that added sorrow to her own fear.

The unicorn turned to Thomas. "What do you make of this, Tinker?"

"It could be just a dream."

"It wasn't!" said Cara indignantly.

The Tinker nodded. "I'll take your word on that. But if it wasn't a dream, then I'm troubled by the question of how Beloved was able to make a connection with you. Something like that can't come out of nowhere. There has to be some contact point, some key."

"Are you carrying anything Beloved might have a connection with?" asked Moonheart sharply.

"I don't think so," said Cara. "Unless . . . could it be the amulet?"

Moonheart snorted a dismissal. "If she could reach you through the amulet, she'd be on her way here already. No, there had to be some other way she made the contact."

"What?" asked Cara, more nervous than ever at this idea. "What could it be?"

"I don't have the slightest idea," said Moonheart, "which is part of what bothers me." Then he made her tell the whole story over again.

When she was done, Moonheart shook his head in dismay. "I can't find the connection." He turned to Thomas. "Will you stay here until morning?"

The Tinker nodded. "Of course."

"Send for me at once if there is any more trouble," said Moonheart. Then he turned and left the clearing.

Thomas stationed himself against the green wall of the hedge. The Squijum curled beside Cara. "We'll be right here if you need us," Thomas assured her.

Even so, after a time the two of them slept.

Cara, however, stayed awake until morning, sometimes closing her eyes but mostly staring up into the clear, star-spattered sky.

Moonheart seemed more cheerful when he returned at sunrise. "Come with me," he told Cara after she had eaten a breakfast of berries. "Finder and Belle will be waiting for us."

"I'll catch up with you later," said Thomas. "I have a bit of business to do before I go. Don't worry," he added reassuringly when he saw the look on Cara's face. "I'll rejoin you. I promise."

With the Squijum bouncing along beside them, they walked for a mile or so through the forest, crossing a stream, then climbing a rocky crest. On the other side of the crest stood Finder and Belle. They nodded and whickered as Cara and Moonheart strode up to them.

"Are you ready to go?" asked Moonheart.

"Certainly," said Belle, while Finder simply nodded.

Cara was always amazed at how quickly a journey could begin here in Luster. At home there would have been a great deal of packing and fussing before such a major expedition could get under way.

Or would there? she wondered as a dim memory of a swift and sudden move made at midnight nudged its way into her mind. With a stab of longing she remembered a little house she had once loved: a house with a climbing tree in the backyard and a good friend next door, a house abandoned in the middle of the night, never to be seen again.

She had cried about that for a time, and then forced it from her mind.

But though she had forgotten it, she now realized she had never really let anyplace feel like home again. Home was someplace you could lose, someplace she did lose every year or so. Letting herself feel at home meant nothing more than setting herself up for another round of grief when it came time to leave.

She had liked the places they had lived; some of them, at least. She had had happy moments in most of them.

But after the little house with the tree, none of them had ever been home again.

One thing that made it easy to set out quickly this time was that the unicorns carried nothing, and expected Cara to travel pretty much the same way. Since it was high summer and the land was laced by clear streams and rich with good things to eat, this was all right with her.

"What about Thomas?" she asked as they set out. "Should we wait for him?"

"He'll find us," said Moonheart. From the tone of his voice, Cara got the feeling that the very fact of Thomas accompanying them was an annoyance Moonheart didn't want to think about.

Cara had spent enough time with the Tinker to know that Moonheart was probably right about Thomas finding them. The man had a knack for showing up in unexpected places. So she set aside her misgivings and made no objection to their setting out.

It was a curiously quiet beginning to their journey.

Well, what did you expect? she thought, chiding herself. *Fanfares? A cheering crowd? These are unicorns; they do things differently. Besides, last night's ceremony was our formal farewell.*

They traveled in silence for a time — not only the silence that comes from not speaking, but the silence of unicorns on the move. The only sound at all was the rustle of leaves beneath Cara's feet as she walked, and an occasional squawk from the Squijum. But the little creature seemed to understand that the unicorns wanted to move without sound for the time being, and so made an effort to restrain his chatter.

As Cara moved into the rhythm of the day, she noticed again how differently time seemed to pass in the wild. In the cities where she had lived it was frantic, divided into little chunks. Here, it seemed to roll on more smoothly.

When the sun was straight overhead, they stopped in a shady glade to rest for a bit. Moonheart used his horn to freshen the water in a small pool, and Cara drank deeply, reveling in its clear, cool flavor. Finder pointed her toward a clump of berry bushes, a kind she had learned to call "sunberries." The bright yellow fruits were small, with a bittersweet taste she had grown quite fond of.

As she was gathering the berries, Finder came to stand at her side. "I've heard many stories about your grandmother," he said in his soft way. "I think she and I have a lot in common."

Cara looked at him in surprise.

"We both like to explore," said Finder, by way of explanation.

Cara had been wondering why someone who seemed so timid had been chosen for the expedition. "Do you explore a lot?" she asked.

"Oh, yes. Often I am the first unicorn to see a place. The unfinished" — Finder broke off, and a heavy silence hung between them for a second until he concluded — "the new places, places where no one has ever been before — they don't bother me the way they do some of us."

He stretched his neck forward and delicately nipped several sunberries from a thorny stem, his muzzle and beard startlingly white against the blue-green leaves. Then he nodded to her and turned to walk away. He whisked his tail as he went. It brushed her arm, feeling like silk at it slid across her skin.

When Cara rejoined the glory, Belle said quietly, "Someone is following us."

"Any idea who it is?" asked Moonheart.

"Not even *what*," said Belle. "Though I doubt delvers could travel that quietly."

Cara looked for the Squijum, thinking perhaps he

could go back to check for them, but the little creature was nowhere to be seen. "Perhaps it's Thomas," she said hopefully.

"Possible," said Belle. "But not likely. He usually makes considerably more racket."

"Keep watch as we travel," ordered Moonheart.

Belle nodded but said nothing.

Their first night they stopped beside a small pond, where Finder showed Cara several things to eat, including a lumpy pod called *skug,* which grew on the roots of one of the water plants. Though the pod looked dreadful, once she had peeled it and washed it in the clear water of the pond, the blue interior proved to be crisp and sweet. She ate a half dozen or so of the pods and felt quite pleasantly full.

She grew nervous as darkness approached, reluctant to sleep for fear Beloved might try to contact her again. But finally the previous night's lack of rest, combined with the exhaustion of the day's journey, proved too much for her, and she nodded off.

The night passed with no repeat of her "dream" of Beloved, and Cara woke feeling both refreshed and enormously relieved.

◆ ◆ ◆

Two days' journeying brought the travelers to the edge of a river that the unicorns called "Diamond Drop." It ran deep and swift, and Cara wondered aloud how they would cross it.

"About an hour upstream we'll come to an easy ford," said Finder, who was standing next to her. And indeed, when they had followed the river for three or four miles, they came to a place where it grew broad and shallow.

Cara thought about undressing before she started across, then decided against it. Even though she couldn't think of any reason *not* to be naked in front of the unicorns, the idea made her uncomfortable. So she took off just her shoes, then waded in. *After all,* she told herself, *it won't take my clothes long to dry. And besides, they could use a good washing.*

The water was crystal clear and, for the most part, no more than a foot or two deep. Cara noticed red fish, as long as her arm, swimming placidly about her feet as she splashed her way across.

When she had nearly reached the far bank, she found a quiet pool, deeper than the water surrounding it. She took advantage of the spot to swim around and clean her clothes a bit.

◆　◆　◆

The day was warm, the sun bright, and it was not long before her clothing dried again. She felt better, and she certainly smelled better. But her long red hair was getting more and more tangled, and she began to think she might never get the knots out of it.

From the river they headed north. After a mile or so of thick forest, they came to a meadow where the waving grass stood nearly as high as Cara's shoulder.

"Would you like to ride?" asked Finder.

"That would be nice," said Cara gratefully. She tried to climb onto his back, but he was so big she had to twine her hands in his mane to pull herself up. He didn't flinch.

She was delighted to be astride a unicorn again. Yet, to her surprise, it made her a little sad, as well. She realized she was missing Lightfoot.

As they started across the meadow, the Squijum gave a squeal of delight and went bounding into the grass, where he disappeared from sight. Cara heard him now and then, shouting, "Hotcha wowie! Bad bug. Wanna eat you!"

Finally his voice faded away altogether.

The meadow was thick with flowers of all shapes and colors, including a purple blossom that grew on a thick stalk and attracted clouds of insects. Their humming filled the air — as did the scent of the blossoms, which was a little like cinnamon. Cara found herself growing drowsy and had to fight to keep herself from falling forward on Finder's back.

Thomas was on the far side of the meadow, leaning against his multicolored cart and whistling casually. The Squijum sat placidly on his shoulder, munching on a biscuit.

"How did you get here?" cried Cara in delight.

The Tinker shrugged. "There are many paths to most places."

"So you weren't the one following us?"

The Tinker looked surprised. "I came from a completely different direction."

"I told you he wasn't the one," said Belle quietly.

"Let's move on," said Moonheart. "We have a lot of ground to cover today."

Thomas picked up the handles of his wagon and fell into place beside the unicorns. The pots, pans, and tools hanging from the roof clattered noisily as he walked.

"Will you quiet that dratted thing down?" snapped Belle after they had gone about a quarter of a mile.

Thomas frowned, then shrugged and turned to the cart. "Shhh!" he hissed.

The pots rattled once, as if annoyed, then fell silent. After that the cart rolled along without a sound, no matter how rugged the terrain they were crossing.

As they traveled, Thomas hummed a melody that was oddly familiar to Cara. Yet she could not figure out where she had heard it before.

The sun was dipping low in the sky when they came to a rocky set of foothills. At the top of the first hill Cara spotted a house. It had a spiky look, caused by at least a dozen turrets and other things — structures she could not identify — sprouting from its roof.

It was startling to see a house here in Luster; in fact, it was the first building she had seen since she'd arrived. "Who lives there?" she asked.

"M'Gama," said a gravelly female voice. The words seemed to come from less than an arm's length away.

Cara turned, but could see no one. "Who said that?" she asked nervously.

"I did," snapped the voice. "And unless you have a good reason for being here, you had best leave now, before *she* turns you all into some very decorative rocks."

CHAPTER FOUR

THE GEOMANCER

Cara put a nervous hand on Finder's shoulder. "Show yourself!" snapped Moonheart. Belle moved into a fighting stance.

At the same time — and somewhat to Cara's surprise — Finder said with a chuckle, "No need for such dramatics. Listen, whoever you are. We come to the Geomancer on the Queen's business."

"Can you prove that?" asked the voice suspiciously.

Moonheart nudged Cara. "Show her the amulet."

Fumbling at the neck of her T-shirt, Cara drew forth the amulet that had carried her into Luster. Its crystal lid caught a ray of the setting sun. Coiled beneath the lid was a luminous strand of white hair.

"That's one of the Queen's Five!" said the voice in surprise.

"Now do you believe us?" asked Finder serenely.

"I suppose I must." As the voice spoke these words, Cara saw some of the rocks beside her begin to shift and change. Within moments she was staring down at a *very* small woman.

"Oh, that *is* clever," said Thomas appreciatively.

The newly revealed dwarf had a high brow and deep-set eyes. She wore a tunic of brown cloth. Her skin was also dusky brown. In one hand she clutched a short spear. Her head reached barely to Cara's waist.

"Follow me," said the dwarf, once she was totally visible. "I will take you to M'Gama." Without another word, she started up the hill, her stubby legs moving so fast that Cara and Thomas were hard put to keep up with her.

The three unicorns, of course, climbed the hill with no problem at all. The Squijum kept racing forward to weave in and out between the woman's feet, until she uttered a burst of angry words and jabbed at him with her spear. He squawked in alarm and scurried back to clamber onto Cara's shoulder. Cara hadn't been able to make out the dwarf's exact words, but she thought she had heard "snack" somewhere among them.

♦ ♦ ♦

Cara was panting when they reached the top of the hill. But though she had to stand with her hand pressed against her side, she was delighted with the house they had come to. From below she had assumed it was built of wood. Now she could see that it was made — all four stories of it — from earth and stone. In fact, from the way the sides merged into the rocky terrain behind it, from up close the dwelling seemed almost to have grown directly out of the hilltop.

Each level of the house was somewhat smaller than the one below, making it look like a stony wedding cake, though not nearly so regular. The main entrance was formed by two tall stones, about four feet apart, with a third placed flat across their tops. The door, also made of stone, stood open.

The dwarf led the way into the house, which was cool and dark inside. Stepping in, Cara felt as if she had entered the hill itself.

Most of the first room was taken up by a stone table on which were scattered bits of earth and rock of all sorts — everything from clots of mud to sparkling gems the size of acorns. A variety of branches stood in a tall, slender pot at one side of the table, some freshly cut, others long dry.

"M'Gama!" cried the dwarf. "We have visitors!"

"Bring them up," replied a voice from somewhere above them.

The dwarf sighed. "Follow me," she said. Then she darted through a door at the back of the room.

Cara wondered how the unicorns felt about being inside — about climbing stairs. But they crossed the room with no comment, their hooves tinkling like silver chimes on the stone floor.

As they passed through the next door Cara saw a room that looked like a kitchen to her left. She didn't have time to study it because the dwarf was urging them up the stairs. These were made of stone as well, the steps being very wide and broad. It took a moment for Cara to realize that they were carved directly into the side of the hill.

The first flight of stairs brought them back into the open, onto a kind of terrace. Remembering how each level of the house was smaller than the one below it, Cara realized they must be standing on the roof of the room they had first entered. The terrace was about ten feet wide, with a stone wall at its edge that reached just to her knees. The Squijum immediately leaped onto the wall and began racing back and forth along it.

Beyond the wall Cara could see the valley they had just traversed. The land rolled on, beautiful and wild, most of it covered with forest. She felt a pang of love for Luster's unspoiled beauty, and ached again at the thought of leaving it.

A gentle nudge from Finder brought her back to the moment, and she realized the unicorns had started up the next level of stairs. Though made of stone like the first level, these were on the outside of the house. They led to another terrace, from which the view was even better.

"Pretty!" said the Squijum happily.

They continued climbing.

"Stairs," Cara heard Belle mutter. "What a stupid idea!"

The final set of steps ended on top of the house. The roof was wide and flat. Open to the valley on one side, it merged directly into the hill on the other. From it sprouted several poles and narrow towers with a variety of whirling arrangements that made Cara think of tiny windmills.

In the center of the roof stood a remarkable-looking woman. Dressed in a flowing robe dyed in deep shades of red, purple, and green, she stood well over six feet tall. The way her hair was piled above her head added several inches to that already considerable height. Her smooth, gleaming skin was nearly jet-black. She had high cheekbones, full lips, and a broad nose. She was astonishingly beautiful — which was somewhat surprising to Cara, who had vaguely been expecting some wizened crone.

"Welcome to my home," said the woman. Her voice was rich and deep. "I am M'Gama, the Geomancer." She gestured toward the dwarf who had escorted them up the stairs. "And this is Flensa. She guards me well."

Cara noticed that while M'Gama's left hand was covered with rings — four or five to each finger — her right hand was bare.

"Guards you from what?" asked Belle.

"From intrusion. From disturbance. From things that would distract me from my study and my work." She closed her eyes for a moment and added, "And from delvers, of course."

"Yike!" yelped the Squijum, leaping onto Cara's leg

and climbing to her shoulder. "Delvers bad. Much not good hotcha phooey!"

"Precisely," said M'Gama, smiling ever so slightly.

"But why would the delvers want to bother you?" asked Cara.

"Because they are earth-creatures. I do not mean," she clarified quickly, "Earth as in the world from which you and I — and the unicorns, for that matter — originally came. I mean creatures of the soil and stone that make up the world. As my magic is earth-magic, there are many things I have that the delvers would like to possess. Tools. Spells. Knowledge. Things I would rather they not take from me. Now, what is it that brings you to my home?"

"We require a reading," said Moonheart.

"Oh, really?" M'Gama raised an elegant eyebrow. "And what would that be for?"

"The child is to return to Earth, to fetch her grandmother, Ivy Morris."

The Geomancer's eyes widened when she heard the name. "So, the Wanderer is going to return to us at last."

She didn't sound entirely pleased at the idea, which

surprised Cara. Everyone else she had met in Luster had been delighted at the thought of the Wanderer returning.

"It is the Queen's wish," said Moonheart sharply.

M'Gama bowed her head. "Then it is my bidding." Extending her right hand, the one bare of jewelry, she said to Cara, "Come, young one. Let us begin the work."

Cara, not entirely sure she wanted to go off with this woman, glanced at Moonheart. At his nod of approval, she stepped forward and took the Geomancer's hand. Together they walked to a door at the back of the roof, which led into the hill itself. Inside was another set of stairs, not so wide as the ones by which Cara had ascended. They started down.

At about the time the light began to fade behind them, the darkness ahead was lessened by a series of clear glass bowls that sat in niches in the wall. Each bowl was filled with a glowing liquid.

As they passed the first bowl, M'Gama dipped a forefinger into the liquid, then painted a line of it across her forehead, where it continued to glow. At the next bowl, she did the same to Cara. The liquid was cool and tingled a bit on her skin.

After another few minutes Cara said, a little nervously, "I don't remember this many steps going up."

M'Gama uttered a low, silky laugh. "Of course you don't. We've gone far below the first level of the house."

"Why?"

"My magic and my study are rooted in the earth. Therefore, I must go into the earth to practice them."

Very deep into the earth, thought Cara as they continued to wind their way down. She tried to count the steps but lost track after the first hundred.

They came at last to a room — a cave, really — crammed with globes, maps, star charts, astrolabes, bubbling retorts, candles with multicolored flames, and pots exuding strange smells. A fire pit carved into the center of the stone floor held a pile of glowing red embers. In the farthest corner stood an intricately carved stone cabinet. Behind its crystal doors Cara could see shelves stacked high with sticks, stones, and clods of moist earth. In front of each item was a card covered with tiny, precise writing. Though the writing was in a language she did not know, Cara had a sense that the cards were labels.

"Pieces of reality," said M'Gama when she noted the

questioning look in Cara's eyes. "These bits of earth are the touchstones of my craft, and the source of my knowledge." She crossed to the fire pit and, in a single, graceful motion, lowered herself so that she was sitting cross-legged on the floor. Patting the stone next to her, she said, "Come and sit beside me. I must learn many things from you before I can do the work that will tell us from where you should depart."

Cara did as the woman asked, imitating her posture. When she was settled, M'Gama extended her right hand and said, "Let me see the amulet."

Cara hesitated a moment, unwilling to let the amulet out of her grasp. But since the Queen had sent her to M'Gama, she decided it must be all right. Slowly, she drew the chain over her head and passed it to the Geomancer.

Rather than look at it, as Cara had expected, M'Gama closed her fingers over the amulet, clenching it so that the chain flowed down from either side of her fist. She closed her eyes and began swaying slowly from side to side. After a moment she crooned a soft, word-less song that reminded Cara of the tune Thomas had been humming earlier that day. Green light began to flow between her fingers — the same green that had shone when the amulet had opened the door to Luster.

Finally M'Gama opened her eyes. "These amulets contain great magic," she murmured, her voice husky. She uncurled her fingers, and the glow vanished. "They hold the power to pierce the walls between worlds, to open a hole from what *is* to what *might be.* Now, tell me where you need to go."

Cara described her home. As she spoke, M'Gama asked many questions. After a while she nodded, then went to one of the globes and began to study it. "You can return to the others now," she muttered, without even glancing up at Cara. "This will take some time."

"Is it all right if I stay?"

"Suit yourself. But please do not speak from this point on."

Sitting in silence, Cara marveled at the cat-like grace with which M'Gama moved around the cave. On a table near the back wall the Geomancer placed several items that she pulled from the cabinet: a smooth, red stone; two long, green feathers; a small bottle of water; and a dried twig. She then took a double handful of dried leaves from a niche in the wall and tossed them onto the embers in the fire pit. Cara gasped as a burst of flame rose from the pit, stretching nearly to the ceiling. But within three or four seconds the fire died down, to be replaced by thick, blue smoke.

As the smoke curled up from the fire pit, it coalesced into a perfect globe that began to turn slowly on its axis. M'Gama sat before the globe, hands on her knees, staring at it as if all the knowledge of the world were somehow concealed beneath its surface.

After a time she began to chant.

A sweet, musky odor filled the cave.

Points of light appeared on the surface of the smoky globe. They began to move, slowly at first, then faster and faster. Soon they looked like lines instead of points. More and more appeared, zipping madly over the globe until it seemed to be made of light instead of smoke.

M'Gama's voice rose higher and higher. "A la manna hayim!" she chanted swaying back and forth. "A la manna hayim!"

Her body began to tremble; suddenly she uttered a shrill cry, then collapsed onto the stone floor.

The globe vanished. The embers were quenched. Even the glowing lines on their foreheads went black, leaving Cara in a darkness so complete it was as if the world itself had disappeared.

CHAPTER FIVE

"I Am Wandering, Wandering . . ."

M'Gama?"

Cara whispered the name, half afraid that someone — or some*thing* — other than M'Gama might answer from the darkness.

When there was no answer at all, she tried again, more loudly. *"M'Gama?"*

Still no answer.

She started to stand, thought better of it, and began to crawl across the floor. The stone was smooth and cool beneath her hands. The air smelled the way it does after a lightning strike.

Hoping she was heading in the right direction, she searched ahead of her with her hands so she would not accidentally come down too hard on M'Gama's body. She continued to whisper the Geomancer's name, wishing M'Gama would respond — if only with a groan — so she would know she wasn't feeling through the dark for a dead woman.

Finally her fingers brushed flesh instead of stone. The moment of shock gave way to relief when she realized the flesh was warm and had flinched slightly at her touch. Scooting forward, Cara rose to her knees and drew the woman's head into her lap. "M'Gama," she whispered urgently. "M'Gama, are you all right?"

The Geomancer shuddered, then took a deep breath. She seemed startled to find Cara holding her, and began to struggle to rise. After a moment she dropped her head back and murmured, "I'll be fine. I just need some time. That was . . . harder than usual."

She fell silent again, though whether she was asleep, unconscious, or merely too tired to speak, Cara wasn't certain. Only the sound of M'Gama's breathing kept the girl from total panic. She felt as alone as she had ever felt, swallowed by the blackness around her.

She closed her eyes to see if it made any difference in the quality of the darkness.

It didn't; the world was equally black either way.

Deprived of sight, her other senses seemed to grow sharper. Somewhere in the distance she heard the slow drip of water. The musky smell of the herbs M'Gama had thrown on the fire lingered around her. She could feel the weave of M'Gama's garment, the threads bold and clear beneath her fingertips.

As time went on, Cara's mind began to wander, tracing back over all that had happened to her since she'd first fallen into Luster. Again she found herself missing Lightfoot and the Dimblethum. She thought with fondness of the Dimblethum's strange face, like that of some bear that had begun to turn into a man, then stopped halfway through the process. Despite his gruffness and his growls he was gentle in his strength.

She never had found out how he and Lightfoot had become friends. She wished Lightfoot was with her now. They had already shared so much danger together it felt strange to be setting out on this adventure without him.

Thinking of the dangers she had shared with Lightfoot inevitably led her to a more disturbing memory . . . that of her father.

She didn't want to miss him, didn't want to love him anymore. But she couldn't stop herself from wondering where he was, if he was all right. Firethroat had said only that she had taken him to a place that was safe, but empty. Was he even now wandering through some wilderness? Wandering like her, only without friends?

She forced the thoughts away. Her father was an enemy of the unicorns, and she could not afford to feel pity or love for him.

In the darkness her mind drifted to her grandmother. She tried to envision her face — something she did almost daily anyway, for fear that if she did not the image might fade from memory. Sometimes, at first, the memory was fuzzy. That always scared Cara. But she found that by focusing on the details, by first recalling the long braid, then the high forehead, the soft skin with its lines like crumpled paper, the gray eyes, the wide mouth, that the picture would sharpen until she saw her grandmother clearly and distinctly once more.

As she did that now, as she began tracing the lines of her grandmother's face in her mind's eye, she thought she heard the old woman singing — a high, thin sound that seemed made up of equal parts of courage and despair.

"Gramma?" she whispered.

The singing continued: "Oh, where's the thread that binds me, the voice that calls me back?" The voice was distant and quavering, but distinct.

"Gramma?" whispered Cara again. "Gramma, where are you?"

"Cara? Cara, is that you? Oh, come and get me, my child. Come and get me. I am wandering, wandering and so far from home."

"Gramma, where are you?"

Her own words, uttered in a desperate cry, came echoing back to her, eerie in the darkness.

But the echoes were all she heard. Her grandmother's voice was gone. Cara strained to hear it again, listening until she thought the black silence would drive her mad. Finally, trembling, she lapsed back into thought. Was she losing her mind? If not, where had the words come from? More importantly: What did they mean?

So absorbed was she in these questions that when someone touched her on the arm she started violently, nearly dropping M'Gama's head to the stone floor.

"*Shhhhh!*" hissed the intruder.

With relief, Cara realized it was Flensa. She could sense the woman next to her, so tiny that though Cara was kneeling and Flensa was standing, the dwarf's mouth was right next to her ear. "This has happened before," whispered Flensa. "Though not often. We must wait."

She sounded angry, as if she blamed Cara for M'Gama's condition. Cara tried to ask a question, but Flensa shushed her again. "Wait," she whispered. "Wait."

After what seemed like hours, M'Gama groaned and stirred again. "Flensa?"

"Here, My Lady."

"Help me to my feet."

"Best to wait a bit, My Lady."

"Then bring me something to drink," said M'Gama, sounding half annoyed, half amused.

Flensa moved away so silently that Cara only knew she was gone by the sudden absence of her body's heat. She wondered how the little woman could see in the dark.

The dwarf returned a few minutes later, something Cara could tell not by her footsteps but by the faintest sound of water sloshing.

"Drink, My Lady," whispered Flensa.

M'Gama moaned, but drank. "Better," she whispered. Reaching behind her, she closed her hand on Cara's arm. "Is that you, child?"

"Yes."

"Are you all right? I am truly sorry if I frightened you."

"I'm all right," said Cara, speaking the truth, though just barely. "But I have to tell you about what happened while you were asleep."

Quickly she spilled out the story of hearing her grandmother's voice, of her strange and desperate words.

"What does it mean?" Cara asked when she was finished. "What does it mean?"

M'Gama was silent for a time. When at last she spoke, her words were of little comfort. "There is a deep strangeness in this. I cannot make sense of it. Was the voice true? I cannot say — though it is certainly possible. A great deal of magic was loose in this cave a little while ago. On the other hand, when one is alone in the dark, the mind can conjure up all sorts of things that have the feel, the seeming, of reality, and yet are not real."

"But what should I do about it?" asked Cara urgently.

"Exactly what you are doing," said M'Gama. "Are you not doing as your grandmother has asked? Are you not in search of her even now?"

"Yes," said Cara. "But I felt as if . . . I don't know . . . as if there was something more my grandmother needed — wanted . . ." Her voice trailed off. "Only I don't know what."

"Then until you do, I think the best thing is to continue the journey you have begun. But keep yourself open, child — always ready to receive what may come. There may be more for you to learn, information that may arrive in unexpected ways."

"I'll try," said Cara, though the idea made her nervous, given the vision of Beloved that she had experienced the night before they'd begun their journey. "How soon can we go back to the others?"

M'Gama laughed. "Give me another few minutes. Flensa, bring some light, please."

The little woman left without a sound. A moment later she returned, carrying one of the bowls of liquid light that had lined the steps leading down to the cave.

The light was low and greenish, but steady, not like the flickering of candles. Shining up into Flensa's face, which was grotesque enough in the daylight, it made the dwarf seem truly eerie. The light was not strong enough to reach the corners of the cave, which remained in shadow.

"Help me to my feet," whispered M'Gama. With Cara's support she was standing by the time Flensa reached them. "All right," she said, taking a deep breath and drawing herself to her full height. "Let us return to the upper world."

Flensa led the way. Though M'Gama had to lean on Cara's shoulder when they started, she seemed to grow stronger by the moment. By the time they had climbed the first twenty or so steps, she released her grip and walked on her own.

Cara stayed close to her, just in case. After another twenty steps she asked softly, "What did you see, M'Gama?"

"When we're out of the caves and with the others I'll tell you. I only want to say it once."

Cara didn't like the sound of that.

◆　◆　◆

By the time they reached the top of the stone stairs, the backs of Cara's legs were aching and she was breathing hard. She saw that it was full dark out — a disappointment, since she had been looking forward to the daylight.

"Oh, well," she muttered as they stepped through the door. "Probably would have hurt my eyes anyway."

"Yowie!" cried the Squijum when he saw them. "Good come back hotcha miss much girl gone too long!" Then he scrambled onto Cara's shoulder and began to tug at her tangled hair.

"Stop it!" she said crossly, too tired and nervous to appreciate his greeting.

"Be nice!" ordered the Squijum, giving her a little smack with his paw. But he settled down, clinging to her shoulder for a full thirty seconds before he darted away again.

"Well?" asked Moonheart. "Were you successful?"

"The work was more difficult than I expected," said M'Gama slowly. "However, I found your answer. Not that you will like it."

"That's encouraging," said Thomas dryly.

"There is nothing here to be taken lightly," snapped M'Gama. "As I walked the lines of the world to look for your answer, I could feel someone trying to find me, trying to discover what I was doing."

"Do you know who it was?" asked Finder nervously.

"Yes. It was the one you call 'Beloved.'"

A coldness rippled across Cara's shoulders. "*Did* she find you?" she asked in horror.

M'Gama shook her head. "I have tricks of my own. But eluding her was . . . unpleasant. As was the answer to your question."

"What do you mean?" asked Finder.

"I have found the place where Cara must make the transfer back to Earth."

"And . . . ?" prompted Moonheart.

M'Gama glanced nervously at the skies. "Let us go below. Some things are best not spoken of in the open."

CHAPTER SIX

PATH TO THE SEVENTH DRAGON

Without another word, M'Gama led them down the broad stone stairs that started on the outside of her home and then, two levels down, shifted inside. The night air was cool, the sky thick with stars. Cara walked beside Finder, her hand on the big unicorn's warm, silky shoulder.

At the main floor they turned and headed into the hill. To Cara's surprise they entered a large chamber — half room, half cave — that could easily have held a dozen unicorns without feeling crowded. It was lit by the same glowing bowls that had lined the stairs Cara and M'Gama had descended to reach the deeper part of the dwelling. Their light filled the center of the chamber but did not reach all the way to the back.

A waterfall ran down the right wall, reminding Cara of how thirsty she was.

"Food and drink for all," said M'Gama, as if she had read the girl's mind. Flensa quickly began bringing bowls from the kitchen that Cara had noticed earlier. The bowls were made of stone. The ones she gave the unicorns were large — so big, the dwarf could barely get her arms around them — and filled with dried flowers.

After watching the dwarf carry in the first bowl, Cara went to help her.

"Where did all this come from?" she asked when they were alone in the kitchen.

"Here and there," said Flensa. "I prepared it while you and my lady were in the earth." She paused, and her face looked troubled. "I also went out to search for any sign of the ones that Belle says are following you. I had to cut short my search when I sensed my lady was in trouble."

Cara looked at the dwarf curiously. "How did you do that?"

Flensa shrugged. "M'Gama and I have a . . . connection."

Cara hoisted one of the bowls, and staggered under the weight. She glanced at the dwarf in surprise, wondering how the tiny woman could carry them so easily.

They arrayed the bowls along a table, which was also made of stone and built at a comfortable height for the unicorns to eat from while standing. Once these bowls were all in, Flensa gestured for Cara to stay in the main hall. She scurried back to the kitchen and returned a moment later with a cart bearing a large black kettle, from which she dished up three helpings of a simmering vegetable stew. The stew seemed to be made mostly of roots; Cara recognized one of the ingredients as *tarka,* something the Dimblethum had taught her to eat.

The Squijum, who had been climbing the stalagmites at the back of the room, came scurrying back. "Food, food! Hotcha wowie much good!" he said, looking for his own bowl. When he realized there wasn't one, Flensa laughed — the first time Cara had heard her make such a sound. Then she produced a final bowl from beneath the cart, a bowl filled with nuts, berries, and uncooked *tarka*.

"Yum!" cried the Squijum, diving at it so ferociously

Cara was afraid he would send the entire contents scattering across the table.

Flensa disappeared back into the kitchen.

"Isn't she going to eat?" asked Cara.

"She prefers to do so alone," replied M'Gama.

They dined in silence for a while. Cara, anxious to hear what M'Gama had learned, had a hard time settling down to eat. But the stew was surprisingly good, and (even more surprising) somehow soothing. *It tastes like home,* Cara decided at last.

Finally M'Gama pushed aside her bowl. "Now we must talk." Raising her voice, she cried, "Flensa! Bring the maps."

A moment later the dwarf scurried in, clutching an armful of scrolls, each almost as long as she was tall. She placed them in front of M'Gama, who sorted through them until she found the one she wanted. After clearing a space on the table, she unrolled the scroll, setting small stones at the corners to hold it in place.

"Look," she commanded.

The company gathered around her, some on the far side of the table, some right next to her. Cara studied the map for a moment, then asked, "Why are there so many blank spaces?"

"Unicorns are neither mapmakers nor land claimers," said Thomas.

"Those are human traits," added Moonheart, with a faint touch of disdain.

M'Gama snorted. "Human traits that are occasionally useful even to unicorns. But Luster is a young world, and has not been deeply explored."

Finder, who had come to stand behind Cara, was poking his big head over her shoulder. "I have been to some of those empty places," he said shyly.

She glanced at him in surprise.

"Why do you think Moonheart asked me to come?" he murmured.

Cara put her hand on his neck, comforted, as always, by his gentle strength.

"Look," said M'Gama, calling Cara's attention back to the map. The place names were written in an ornate script that she could not read, but M'Gama whispered them aloud as she traced the path they must follow with her fingertip.

"You'll start here, at my home," said the Geomancer

softly. "Travel west for five days, until you come to the River Silver, which flows down from the north."

"Grimwold's territory is somewhere around there, isn't it?" asked Moonheart.

"It is," replied M'Gama. "At least, the outer edges of it. If I can contact him, I'll let him know that you are heading in his direction."

The thought pleased Cara. Grimwold was the Keeper of the Unicorn Chronicles, and though he was a bit cantankerous, she had grown fond of him on her first visit to his caves — partly because he had known her grandmother from the time she was as young as Cara herself was now.

"Once you reach the Silver, you must move carefully, for you will be skirting delver territory. Follow the river north, until you come to a forest. You will pass through wooded areas along the way, of course, but you will know this forest when you see it, for it rises abruptly from a stretch of flat grassland and stretches like a wall for as far as you can see in either direction. This stage of the journey will take you several days."

"Can you be more precise?" asked Thomas.

"Not really. The river winds and twists and sometimes shifts in its course. If the water is high, you may find yourself making lengthy detours. Even so, it is the only good way through this territory. It will take at least ten days."

"It seems like such a long way," said Cara. "And not anywhere near where I entered Luster."

"That's because the world has shifted since you first came here," said M'Gama. "It will shift again, before too long. Autumn is approaching, and the days are growing shorter. On the day when the light and the dark are in balance, this spot will cease to be of use to you."

Cara felt a twist of fear. "How much time do we have?" she asked urgently.

M'Gama closed her eyes, as if consulting some internal calendar. "The shift will occur as the sun sets on the thirty-first day of your journey."

"Does that give us enough time to get there?"

"It depends on what happens along the way. It also depends on what happens once you cross over to Earth. If the Wanderer is waiting and you can turn around and come right back, that is one thing. But remember, the connection works both ways. Once the shift occurs, the place I am sending you will no longer take you to your old home. And if you have already gone through, using the amulet to return from Earth will not bring you back to that spot."

"Where will it bring me back to?" asked Cara nervously.

"I do not know. Therefore, I suggest you try your hardest to return before the shift occurs. Now, let me finish giving you the directions." Again she drew their attention to the map. "Once you reach the forest you must be extremely cautious. There is an enchantment on the woods that makes it hard to pass through them. If you go the wrong way, you may find yourself wandering in circles without ever finding the way out." She dropped her voice to a whisper. "Ever," she repeated darkly.

"Then how do we get through them?" asked Cara.

"There is a true path, which will guide you safely as long as you stick to it. The entrance is marked by a pair of black stones, each twice as tall as a unicorn, that stand about an armspan apart. You will find them a half day's journey to the east of where the river enters the forest. Take that path all the way through the forest."

"Wait a minute," said Thomas nervously. "Doesn't that path lead to . . ."

M'Gama finished the sentence for him. "It will take you to the Northern Waste that is home to the seventh dragon."

"Yike!" cried the Squijum. He jumped onto Finder's shoulder, causing the big unicorn to flinch.

"Who is the seventh dragon?" asked Cara.

"Ebillan!" whispered Thomas. The dismay in his voice frightened Cara, who had come to count on the Tinker as being sure and steady no matter how bad the situation.

M'Gama turned to Cara. "Seven dragons came from old Earth to Luster. Their names, in the order of their arrival, are Firethroat, Redrage, Fah-Leing, Master Bloodtongue, Graumag, Bronzeclaw, and Ebillan. Of these seven, Ebillan is the smallest but also the most unpredictable, which makes him one of the most dangerous. He is heartsore and angry, and bears little love for humans — dangerous traits in a dragon. Even so, it is to his home that you must travel."

"By 'home,' I hope you mean simply the territory that Ebillan controls," said Thomas.

M'Gama shook her head. "No, I mean his home. At the back of Ebillan's cave is a smaller cave. Its walls are made of crystal, and he allows none to enter it."

"Then how am I going to get in?" asked Cara.

"That is not a question I can answer. I can only tell you that if you stand in that cave to use the amulet, it should take you directly to your old home."

"*Should?*" echoed Cara nervously. She would have preferred a nice, definite *will*.

"That is what my geomancing told me. Can I make a guarantee? Of course not. Very little is certain in this life. Sometimes you simply have to do, and hope."

CHAPTER SEVEN

THE BATHING
POOL

Cara felt safe in M'Gama's house. Even so, she slept fitfully that night. In her dreams she stood in her grandmother's bedroom and wept, though she could not tell who — or what — it was that she wept for.

She was roused from her troubled sleep by the morning sun peeking over the edge of the second-floor terrace. Her first movements brought a sputter of protest from the Squijum, who was curled at her side with his tail tucked over his eyes.

When Cara stumbled down the stone steps to the main floor, she found the Geomancer standing at the table in the entry room. The table was no longer covered by bits of earth and stone, but held instead an array of clothing.

"You should be better outfitted before you continue your journey," said M'Gama. "Unicorns tend not to think about these things. Also, you should let me help you with your hair."

Cara put her hand to her head. Her thick red hair, usually so neatly groomed at home, was not only tangled but becoming matted. "You're not going to cut it off, are you?" she asked nervously.

M'Gama laughed. "It might be a good idea. But for now we'll simply get it in shape for traveling. Flensa will help you first. I'll join you in a while."

As if summoned by the very mention of her name, the dwarf appeared at Cara's side. "Follow me," she growled. Turning, she led Cara back to the hall where they had dined the night before. She stopped to pick up one of the glowing bowls and motioned for Cara to do the same. This done, they headed toward the back of the chamber, the area that had remained in darkness the night before. Cara could see now that the cave tapered to a narrow opening that seemed to tunnel straight into the hill. The stalactites hanging from the ceiling and the stalagmites thrusting up from the floor looked like giant teeth, giving the tunnel itself the appearance of a long, dark throat waiting to swallow her.

"Where are we going?" Cara asked, fighting to keep the tremor out of her voice.

"You'll see," grunted Flensa.

Though Cara found picking her way among the rocky formations into the dark tunnel somewhat nerve-racking, the traveling was smooth once they entered it. The tunnel sloped downward for a good distance, bringing them at last to a cave lit by several more glowing bowls. The air was cool and moist, making Cara think of the cellar under the little house with the climbing tree back on Earth.

In the center of the cave was a stony pool. Steam drifted across its still surface, much as it does above a pond on a crisp autumn morning. The sound of slowly dripping water echoed around them, bouncing eerily off the cave walls.

"You can bathe here," said Flensa.

Cara waited for the dwarf to leave, but after a moment it became clear that she had no intention of going. Cara hesitated, then, telling herself not to be silly, undressed. Bracing herself for a shock of coldness, she stepped gingerly into the water. "It's warm!" she cried in delight.

Flensa waited until Cara's voice had finished bouncing off the walls before she replied, "What did you expect?"

Cara had never dreamed a hot bath could feel so good. She swam across the pool. It was about ten feet wide and so deep her feet could not touch bottom in the middle. She clung to the far side for a moment, then swam back to the ledge where she had first stepped into the pool. The echoes of her splashing were a little eerie, and yet at the same time somehow comforting.

"This is wonderful," she sighed, leaning against a place where the stone was polished to a smooth sheen. "I wish — what are you *doing?*"

"These herbs are good for your skin," said Flensa as she dumped a double handful of dried leaves into the pool. "Stir them around."

Cara did as she was instructed. At first, the addition to the water made her skin tingle in an unpleasant way. But after a minute or two, the sensation vanished and a spicy odor filled the warm, moist air.

After a while M'Gama came to join them. She helped Cara wash her hair, then massaged a dark blue concoction into it. The earthy smell of the stuff was intense, yet somehow soothing. M'Gama sang as she worked. When the song was finished, she said, "Now rinse it out."

Cara had to duck her head under the warm water of the pool several times before all the stuff was gone. Once it was, M'Gama patted the stone next to her and said, "Now come sit with me."

Cara took the towel Flensa handed her, wondering as she did where it had come from. It was coarse, obviously handwoven, but surprisingly soft. After drying herself, she wrapped the towel around her and went to sit beside M'Gama.

The Geomancer showed her a comb made from dark wood, its ornate handle carved like a dragon. "A friend made this for me," she said as she began to untangle Cara's hair.

It took nearly two hours, some strange-smelling lotions, and (Cara suspected) a bit of magic to get all the knots out. After the first ten minutes, Cara began to grow restless. "We have to hurry!" she said at last. "I have to get moving."

"Yes, you do," replied M'Gama serenely. "But the journey ahead of you calls for endurance as much as speed, and you will do better — last longer — if you set off rested and well prepared. Haste at the start often costs much more time at the end. Turn your head to the right, please."

Cara took a breath and tried to settle herself. Despite her eagerness to begin the journey, she managed to relax a bit, and to listen.

As M'Gama manipulated the comb, she spoke of her work as Geomancer and how she had come to learn the rhythms of the world and the shape of the stones. She told of the lines of power that run beneath the surface of all worlds, and the secrets that can be read in a pebble, a leaf, a twig, or a clod of soil. As Cara listened she felt the world opening up to her, expanding, as if she could see it in a new way. Sometimes rather than speaking aloud, M'Gama would whisper. Three times she sang — secret songs, which could only be uttered *inside* the world, in a cave, as they were now.

When she was done with the combing, she plaited Cara's hair into two thick braids. "This will help keep it from tangling again. Now come. The others are waiting."

Cara put on her clothes, which felt grubby against her clean skin, and followed Flensa and M'Gama out of the cave.

◆　◆　◆

"Oh, well done!" said Thomas, who was lounging near the front door. "Your hair looks very good that way."

"Thank you," said Cara, blushing a little. Then, quickly, she added, "M'Gama did it."

"Come, child," said M'Gama, who was standing at the table once more. "We are not finished yet. Let us see if any of these will fit you."

"Where did this all come from?" asked Cara as she examined the variety of clothing spread out on the table.

The Geomancer turned her palms upward. "People sometimes come to me for information. When they do, they offer me something in return, usually something they have made. I take whatever they offer. You never know when something will come in handy."

"How many humans are there in Luster, anyway?" asked Cara, picking up a pair of leather trousers. She held them to her waist, then sighed and put them back since they were at least a foot too long for her.

M'Gama paused. "Not very many. I suspect if you gathered us all together you might have enough to make a medium-sized town. Of course, I speak only of this continent. What is over the sea, I cannot say. Here, try this on."

By the time they were done, Cara was outfitted in a loose linen shirt covered by a dark green tunic woven from some fabric she did not recognize; a pair of close-fitting brown trousers that were far easier to move in than her jeans had been; and a pair of high boots made of supple, earth-colored leather. Better yet, M'Gama gave her a pack in which she was able to carry two additional sets of clothing.

"Best take this cloak, too," said the Geomancer, rolling another piece of fabric and tucking it into the pack. "You'll be traveling north, and summer is coming to its end. Evenings may be cool."

To finish the outfit, she strapped a short sword to Cara's side. "May you never have to use it," whispered the Geomancer. "But may it perform its job well if you do."

Cara drew the sword and stared at it, feeling a strange mixture of excitement and fear. Somehow having an adult give her a such a weapon made the dangers of the path ahead seem even more real.

"I wish I could have some lessons," she muttered.

"With luck, you won't need it for anything more

than slicing a path through the underbrush," said M'Gama. "Let us rejoin the others."

Feeling more prepared to face her task than she had at any point since her meeting with the Queen, Cara followed M'Gama to where the unicorns were waiting.

"What a transformation!" said Belle appreciatively. "You look much more suited for a fight."

"Much more suited to travel and explore," corrected Finder, earning himself a scowl from Belle.

Moonheart stepped forward. "On behalf of the Queen, I thank you for your help, M'Gama. I will report to her when we return."

"Assuming we do return," said Finder, in a voice solemn enough that Cara knew he wasn't joking.

Moonheart was clearly eager to be moving, a feeling that matched Cara's perfectly, so the good-byes were quick. Yet despite her eagerness to be on the road, when Cara turned to leave she suddenly realized how good it had been to be inside a house, even one as odd as M'Gama's, even if for only a day. Breaking from the group, she ran back to the Geomancer and threw her arms about her waist. "Thank you," she whispered. "For everything."

"You are welcome, child," whispered M'Gama,

stroking the top of her head. "For your sake, if not for the sake of the Wanderer, I wish you success on your journey." She hesitated for a moment, then slipped her hand into her pocket. "I want you to take this," she said, holding out a ring made of green stone that had been polished until it was smooth as glass.

"I can't —"

"Take it!" said M'Gama fiercely. "And may you travel in safety."

"Thank you," said Cara softly. She turned to Flensa, who was standing slightly behind M'Gama. Her ugly little face was set in a deep scowl, and she was clutching her spear as if ready to use it. "My thanks to you, too," Cara said softly.

Flensa nodded but said nothing. Cara rejoined the unicorns, and they started west, away from M'Gama's home, and toward the River Silver.

They had not been traveling for more than an hour when Belle suddenly broke away from the group and trotted back the way they had come.

"Where's she going?" asked Cara.

"Hard to say," replied Finder, who was walking beside her. "Belle is not one to talk. Mostly she just *does*. But she'll be back."

And indeed, in less than ten minutes she returned and said softly, "Someone is following us again."

Moonheart looked concerned. "Do you have any idea who it is?"

Belle shook her head, causing her mane to flow like foamy water over her graceful neck. "The signs are very subtle. Whoever it is knows how to be careful."

"We'll have to do the same," said Moonheart.

And with that they started moving again, faster than before.

"I don't like this," said Cara nervously.

"Fear not, fair lady," said Thomas. He took out one of his watches, wound it, then returned it to a different pocket. "We travel with the best the Queen has to offer." He took out another watch and began to fiddle with it, trying to look casual. Even so, he had sounded slightly nervous himself.

The path they followed was so faint that Cara could scarcely detect it. The unicorns claimed that the signs were clear. Even so, Cara noticed that Moonheart let Finder take the lead for most of this stage of the journey.

When they camped the first night, Cara searched

until she found a smooth stick, thick as her thumb and about a foot long. Then she carved a notch at one end.

"What's that?" asked Thomas, who had been watching her.

"My calendar," she replied. She ran her thumb over the notch. "We have thirty days left."

She tucked the stick into her pack.

Late in the afternoon of the third day Cara noticed a bell-like sound somewhere ahead of them. "Do you hear that?" she asked Thomas.

The Tinker set down the handles of his cart and furrowed his brow, seeming to concentrate fiercely. Suddenly a broad smile creased his face. "I do!"

"Well, what is it?"

"Either a very strange bird, or Armando."

"Wonderful," muttered Moonheart. "Armando. Exactly what we need!" With a snort of disgust, he trotted to the front of the group.

"Who's Armando?" asked Cara after Moonheart was gone.

Thomas raised one eyebrow. "Patience, my child. Anticipation is half the fun in a surprise!"

Cara made a little growl, but said nothing more. They were walking through a sun-dappled stretch of forest, still following the faint path Finder had said was the best route to the River Silver. The air was clean and sweet. The first hints of autumn were tinting the leaves with blue and silver. The occasional song of a bird — a real bird, not the strange sound she had heard earlier — drifted through the forest. When it did, Thomas would name the bird for her and tell her what Earth bird it was most like, or what made it unique to Luster.

Despite her urgent desire to reach her grandmother, she was enjoying the journey — partly because they were making good time, which eased her nervousness. But now she found that in addition to the nagging fear that was always present at the back of her mind, she was subject to a gnawing curiosity — a curiosity that continued to grow as they traveled since the sounds ahead were becoming louder and more interesting. Cara heard bursts of music, occasional laughter, shouts of delight, and — once — a cry of pain.

At last they topped a small rise and, looking down into the clearing before them, Cara saw the source of the mysterious sounds.

CHAPTER EIGHT

THE QUEEN'S PLAYERS

Standing in the center of the clearing was a short, chubby man dressed in outlandish clothing. "Welcome, friends!" he cried. "The Queen's Players salute you!"

Then he tumbled forward and stood on his head.

At the far side of the clearing were three gaily colored wagons, much like Thomas's. Clustered between the wagons and the man standing on his head were nearly two dozen oddly assorted people.

Cara, startled by the size of the group, thought, *That's more humans than I've seen since I entered Luster!*

The people were dressed in bright, fanciful clothing, ornamented with bows, ribbons, and plumes. Some of the men wore tight-fitting outfits, checkered with a pattern of large black and yellow diamonds. Others wore flared pants and white silk shirts. One of the women was dressed to look like a cat.

One of the men in black tights came running toward the headstander, did two handsprings, then vaulted over the chubby man's skyward-pointing feet.

"Well done!" cried Thomas, applauding. "Oh, *well* done!" At the same time, the Squijum scurried over to the upside-down man, leaped onto his belly, and began digging into his pockets.

"Wait, wait, *wait!*" giggled the man, tumbling back to the ground, where he lay shaking with laughter.

"Hotcha gotcha!" cried the Squijum, pulling a morsel of something from the man's pocket. "Hotcha gotcha, Armando!"

"Stand up, old friend," said Thomas. "I have someone I want you to meet."

The little man scrambled to his feet, brushed himself off, and did his best to look dignified — not easy with the grin that kept twitching at the corners of his mouth and the merry look that sparkled in his eyes. His efforts were not aided by the Squijum, who was sitting on his neck and tickling his ear with one paw.

"All right, Thomas," said the man. "Introduce your companion. The arrival of another two-legs in Luster is always interesting news."

At a gesture from Thomas, Cara stepped forward. In a formal voice, the Tinker said, "Cara Diana Hunter, allow me to present you to Armando de la Quintano, head of the Queen's Players."

The little man looked momentarily startled when he heard her name. But he quickly got his face under control. "Delighted to meet you!" he cried, sweeping forward in a bow that tumbled the Squijum onto the ground before him. Ignoring the creature's indignant squawks, Armando asked, "And what brings you on this rather remote path?"

Moonheart came to stand beside Cara. "We travel on a mission from the Queen," he said.

"What a coincidence!" cried Armando. "So do we!"

"Ours is considerably more urgent," replied Moonheart sourly. "Which means we have little time for foolery."

"More's the pity, for we are little more than fools. Even so, if we are going in the same direction, perhaps we can travel together for a bit." Reaching above him,

Armando plucked a purple flower from the seemingly empty air. With a bow, he handed it to Cara.

Blushing slightly, she tucked it behind her ear.

"We are heading for the River Silver," said Moonheart.

"Good gracious!" cried Armando. "So are we!"

This news was so exciting that three of the people behind him stood on their heads, and five others turned somersaults.

"Pack up!" bellowed Armando. "Moonheart and his friends are in a hurry, and we cannot delay them."

Moonheart's handsome face twisted into a scowl. Finder moved close to him and spoke gently, words that Cara could not hear. Moonheart nodded and seemed to relax a little. Belle stood aloof from the Players. Finder, on the other hand, plunged in among them as soon as he left Moonheart's side. From the sounds of their greetings to the big gentle unicorn he was both well known and well loved.

Soon enough they were traveling again, though nowhere near as silently as usual. That was all right with Cara. She didn't mind the extra noise as long as the Players didn't slow them down.

She found herself walking between two of the black-clad men. After a few minutes they glanced at each other over her head, nodded, then shouted, "Hup!" Before she could say a word of protest, they had hoisted her onto their shoulders, where they carried her for the next fifteen minutes.

The Players sang as they traveled, sometimes the whole company belting out a marching song that made Cara's feet want to move at a faster pace, other times a single voice offering a song. Some of these solos were so sad that Cara's eyes brimmed with tears, making Luster go blurry around her. Others were so funny that she found herself laughing out loud.

The sound of her own laugh startled her at first. When she tried to figure out why, she realized it was because she had not laughed since that heartbreaking meeting with her father in Firethroat's cave. She felt a little guilty about the laugh — wondered if it was all right for her to do so when she still carried such sorrow. But the bumptious humor of the songs was proof against such reasoning, and forced her to laugh again and again, whether she wanted to or not.

By the time they stopped to make camp Cara had

had a chance to meet several members of the troupe. They were the oddest assortment she had ever come across: people who had come to Luster from all corners of Earth, and from a variety of times. Yet for all their differences, they had a number of things in common — including a deep love of what they did and an obvious joy in the world around them.

From one of them, a petite woman named Li Yun, Cara learned more of how the Players operated.

"The Queen herself has charged us to wander Luster, fooling, tumbling, and singing for both humans and unicorns," the woman told her. "We put on plays and shows of all sorts, everything from dramas, where we act out important stories from the Unicorn Chronicles, to evenings that consist of nothing but singing, juggling, and general foolery."

"What do *you* do?" asked Cara.

Li Yun smiled. "I am an acrobat," she said — then did a series of flips to prove it.

Later, Cara walked beside an older man name Jacques, who had sunken eyes and a deeply seamed face. Despite his melancholy look, he told her a nonstop stream of jokes that sometimes had her doubled over with laughter. He always seemed surprised when she laughed, and never displayed the least hint of a smile himself. The more solemn he remained, the funnier his jokes seemed.

The second night, the Players put on a show for Cara and the unicorns. Cara sat enthralled as they juggled flaming torches, hurled themselves about the clearing like living cannonballs, and clowned with such hilarious abandon that even Moonheart could be heard to laugh on occasion — usually nothing but a low nicker, though once he startled everyone with a loud bray of amusement.

One of the wagons had a side that folded down to make a theater for puppetry. They used this for a comic story about a bandit and a unicorn, and again later for a strange and unexpectedly moving piece about a rock and a river arguing over whether it was better to roam the world or stay in one place.

To close the show, the old man called Jacques stood alone in front of a fading campfire and sang a haunting song that pierced Cara's heart. She recognized the melody at once; she had recently heard bits of it from

M'Gama and Thomas. But it was the words of the chorus that made her shiver.

> *My heart seeks the hearth,*
> *My feet seek the road.*
> *A soul so divided*
> *Is a terrible load.*

She had heard them before — not here in Luster, but back on Earth, and always late at night. They had been sung by her grandmother when she'd thought Cara was sleeping. Now Cara was a Wanderer, too — wandering in search of her grandmother. *And what else?* she asked herself.

Answers, she decided. *I want answers.*

And deeper in her heart, in a place so sore she was not willing to look at it, a voice whispered, *I want to know who loves me.*

She felt a tear trickling down her cheek and lifted her hand to wipe it away.

To her astonishment, the ring M'Gama had given her was glowing. Forgetting her sorrow, she stared at it. But even as she watched, the glow faded, and the ring went dark again.

♦ ♦ ♦

Shortly after noon of the next day they reached the River Silver, a broad strip of water that did indeed look like a band of silver in the bright sunshine. Cara stared at it in wonder, realizing she had never seen a river this clear back on Earth.

Here the Players and the unicorns had to part company. Before they made their final farewells, Cara sought out Jacques and said, "Would you sing that song for me again — the one you sang last night."

He shook his head. "I don't think so. The 'Song of the Wanderer' is for —"

"Is that the name of the song?" interrupted Cara eagerly.

Jacques looked surprised. "Of course. Didn't I mention that when I sang it? No, maybe I didn't. Everyone in the troupe knows it so well, it didn't even occur to me to say what it was. Anyway, it's not a song I sing very often. Reminds me too much of the one I learned it from. I don't know why I sang it for you. Maybe because you're on a journey yourself it seemed appropriate somehow."

"Who taught it to you?" asked Cara.

The lines that etched Jacques' face seemed to grow

even deeper. "I learned it from the Wanderer herself. Her name was Ivy Morris."

Moving close, looking into his dark eyes, Cara whispered, "Ivy Morris is my grandmother."

Jacques stared at Cara in astonishment. Then, narrowing his eyes, he said softly, "Yes. Yes, I can see it! Wait here a moment. I'll be right back."

He hurried to Armando and whispered in his ear. The ringmaster's usually merry face darkened to a scowl. Jacques whispered again, his face urgent. Finally Armando's shoulders slumped, and he spread his hands in a gesture of defeat. Then he stepped forward and embraced Jacques tightly.

When Jacques finally disentangled himself from Armando, he went to Moonheart. At the old clown's first words, the unicorn shook his head from side to side. Jacques continued to speak, the urgency of his words showing in his face. Soon Finder joined them; after a minute or so, the big unicorn began to speak himself, addressing his words to Moonheart.

Finally Moonheart nodded his agreement. But he didn't look happy.

Jacques, on the other hand, was ecstatic. With an

unusual smile creasing his lined face, he hurried to Cara and said happily, "I'm coming with you!"

"Why? I mean . . . I'm sorry, I don't mean to —" She felt herself blush at the rudeness of her question.

Jacques lifted a hand to silence her. Then he knelt, took both her hands in his, and looked directly into her eyes. "I'm coming because I want to help you on your journey."

"But why?" asked Cara again.

His gaze grew more intense. "I have many reasons. But one among them should be enough."

"What is it?" she asked, starting to feel nervous.

Though the old man was still smiling, Cara could see tears welling up in his eyes. Squeezing her hands, he said softly, "I want to come along because I'm your grandfather."

CHAPTER NINE

FIGHT IN THE FOREST

Cara blinked and stepped backward, too startled to reply at first. When she did catch her breath, she said, "What are you talking about?"

Jacques rose to his feet, a hurt look in his eyes. "I thought you'd be pleased."

Cara didn't know what to say. A thousand questions were tumbling through her head, each clamoring to be answered. Was it possible this was true? If not, why would Jacques tell such a story? But if it was, why had her grandmother never mentioned this man? Cara realized, with shock and a little sadness, how little she really knew of her grandmother's past life.

Jacques was still looking at her. In her confusion, she blurted, "But I've never even heard of you!"

The sorrow in his eyes made her wish she could take back the words. After a moment, he said softly, "The wedding of the Wanderer to Jacques the Tumbler is recorded in the Chronicles." He paused again, then added, "Do you know about the Unicorn Chronicles?"

Cara nodded. "I've been to Grimwold's cavern. But I thought he only kept track of stories."

"Our wedding *was* a story," replied Jacques, somewhat ruefully. "A day of celebration and catastrophe. However, even if that were not true, it would have been recorded in Grimwold's cave, for he keeps lists of marriages, births, and deaths for all the humans in Luster."

"No wonder he's so busy!"

"Oh, there aren't that many of us. It's the adventures of the unicorns that really keep him busy. Anyway, you'll find our marriage listed there. Now, it is possible that after Ivy returned to Earth —" Jacques broke off, a pained expression twisting his features, and turned away from her for a moment. "I suppose it is possible you are not my blood granddaughter," he whispered. When he turned back to her his face was calmer. "That makes no difference to me. You are the grandchild of Ivy Morris. I was once the husband of Ivy Morris. As far as I am concerned, that makes you my grandchild."

Suddenly Cara realized that the unicorns had not told the Players the true nature of their quest. "Do you know what we're doing?" she asked softly. "Where we're going?"

Jacques shook his head.

"I am returning to Earth . . . in order to fetch my grandmother back to Luster."

A stricken look crossed Jacques' face. "Are you sure the Wanderer *wants* to return?"

"The last thing Gramma Morris said to me before I jumped into Luster was, 'Find the Old One. Tell her'" — Cara faltered for a moment, just as her grandmother had, then went on — "'Tell her, "The Wanderer is weary."'"

Jacques nodded. "Then she is ready to come back." In his voice Cara heard such an odd mixture of relief and sorrow, hope and pain, longing and anger, that she could make no sense of it.

"Why did Gramma go back to Earth to begin with?" she asked urgently. "I wouldn't have if I were her. I wouldn't now, if I didn't have to get her. I love it here."

"As did she," replied Jacques. "But what you love and what you feel you must do are sometimes different things. More than that, I cannot say. It is your grandmother's story. I will not tell it for her."

Cara rolled her eyes, but Jacques caught her hand and said urgently, "I know that is frustrating to hear. But this is a matter of honor and trust. It is not my story to tell."

Cara held herself stiff for a moment, then relaxed. "All right," she said. "I understand."

Which was almost true.

When the other Players learned Jacques was leaving them, there was a great deal of hugging and crying that had to be accomplished before they would let him depart.

Finder stood next to Cara while this was going on. "Look at Moonheart," the big unicorn whispered.

Cara glanced over at their leader. His nostrils were flared, his eyes hard, his mouth set in a grimace of annoyance.

"He doesn't like sentimental good-byes," said Finder.

When the farewells were finally over, the two groups headed their separate ways. As they walked north along the riverbank, Cara listened to the singing of the Players grow dim behind them; even after the last voices had faded, she could hear the slight *boom* of their drum.

Finally even that was gone.

She looked around her and smiled. What an odd group they made! Three unicorns, three humans, and a Squijum. Even in her wildest daydreams back on Earth she had never imagined that someday she would be trekking across another world, a world of unicorns, in such company. But maybe this was the life of a Wanderer — or at least the granddaughter of a Wanderer.

Her thoughts were interrupted by the Squijum, who came bouncing up from behind, scrambled onto her shoulder, and began chattering in her ear.

She walked beside Jacques off and on during the day, drawn to him, but distrustful as well. It was as if her heart was at war with itself: part of it wanting to accept him at once as her grandfather; another part holding back, fearful, thinking only that here was one more person who could abandon her, betray her.

For his part, he looked sad each time she stepped away from him — or, more precisely, sadder than usual, since his normal look was one of melancholy. That changed whenever she returned to his side. Then his eyes would brighten, and a smile would struggle, briefly, across his well-creased face.

They did not talk much, though late in the day she began to tell him some of the adventures that had befallen her since she'd crossed into Luster. He listened solemnly, and once put his arm around her shoulder and drew her to him, as if wishing he had some way to ease her memories.

Their path took them upward for most of the day. By the time they emerged from the woods into a high, rocky area, Cara's legs were aching. The afternoon sun was dropping lower in the sky to their left when the travelers began to follow a track that led along the edge of a drop so deep it made Cara uneasy to look at the river below.

Evening was falling fast as the path dipped into forest once again. It was much darker under the trees than it had been in the open, and the travelers had gone only a little way into the woods when they decided they should stop for the night.

Cara was glancing around for a good resting place when she head something rustling in the darkness. She reached for Finder. A twig snapped somewhere off to her right.

"What was —"

Her words were cut off by a hideous screech as a band of delvers burst from the underbrush. They were only about three feet tall, but there were well over a dozen of them, all clutching short spears. In the dim light their enormous eyes seemed almost to glow in their oversized heads.

Immediately the three unicorns positioned themselves around the humans. At the same time, Cara put her hand to the blade M'Gama had given her. Her heart pounded with fear. She had been attacked by a delver only moments after she'd first arrived in Luster and she remembered too clearly the feeling of the little monster's wiry hands around her throat.

The delvers rushed forward. Cara's fear turned to stark terror when they began chanting, *"Get her! Get her! Get her!"*

The unicorns reared and kicked, their cloven hooves slashing through the air like silvery knives.

The first blow was struck by Moonheart, who caught one of the delvers on the shoulder. With a shriek, the murderous creature dropped his spear and staggered back.

The other delvers fell away for a second, then rushed forward again. Shrieking louder than ever, they jabbed viciously at the unicorns' bellies with their spears.

Belle spun and kicked backward, sending two of the screaming monsters into the brush.

Cara watched, trembling with terror, rage, and frustration. The Squijum, clinging to her neck, cried encouragement to the unicorns: "Gittem, gittem, gittem! Hittem, unicorns! Hittem *hard!*"

Beside her, Thomas was fumbling with one of his many watches, muttering angrily to himself about not being better prepared. Jacques had drawn a knife from his tunic. He kept trying to position himself to protect Cara, but that was almost impossible since the delvers were attacking from all sides.

Cara drew her sword. The hilt was cold in her hand. She held it before her, ready to slash, wishing desperately that she knew more about using it.

Suddenly the manikins set up a weird cry, a piercing ululation that was one of the most horrifying sounds she had ever heard. She dropped her blade and clapped her hands to her ears, trying to shut out the delvers' screeching, which seemed to slice into her like a living knife. She could see the unicorns shaking their heads violently, as if trying to drive the cries from their ears.

A half dozen of the delvers stopped chanting. While the rest continued their weird cries, these six tightened their grips on their spears and started forward. Belle trumpeted in rage. Dashing toward them, she struck one down with her hooves.

The others fell back. But the horrible chanting continued and Cara could see that it was making it hard for the unicorns to focus on the battle.

"Aha!" cried Thomas in sudden triumph. "*This* should do the trick." Fingers working frantically, he wound one of his many watches, then held it up and flipped open the lid.

As if sound itself had vanished from the world, a complete and utter silence fell over the battle. The delvers looked so baffled — their huge eyes goggling in shock as their mouths moved, but produced no sound — that Cara couldn't help but laugh.

To her astonishment, no sound came from her own mouth, either.

Thomas winked at her. The unicorns took advantage of the delvers' surprise to rush at them. The silence of the fighting that followed — the absolute lack of cries of anger or shrieks of pain, of trumpets, whinnies, or shouts, of even the sound of feet and hooves — was eerie. Cara couldn't even hear the Squijum, though he was still on her shoulder, shaking his paws at the enemy and clearly shouting all sorts of scathing insults.

For a time it looked as if the unicorns would win. Their flying feet and snapping mouths — more vicious in battle than Cara would have thought possible — kept the enemy at bay. But they were hampered by fighting in the woodland, where the obstructing trees gave an advantage to their small foes.

Then Finder stumbled — tripped over a delver, actually — and fell to the ground. This was all the delvers needed. In an instant they were swarming over the big unicorn like ants on a sweet. And in the silence created by Thomas's spell, neither Belle nor Moonheart could hear his desperate whinnies, nor Cara's cry of rage and horror.

Snatching up her blade from where she had dropped it when the delver chant had begun, Cara raced forward to help Finder. Before she could reach him, more delvers burst through the opening created by

Finder's fall and began leaping to attack Belle and Moonheart.

Cara lashed out with her blade. Despite her lack of training, her first swing struck home. The feel of the blade as it entered delver flesh, the spurt of green blood, made her stomach turn. But her rage at these creatures who attacked her and her friends overwhelmed the fear and disgust.

With a ferocious cry she pulled her blade free. Two other delvers took the place of the one she had struck down. She swung at them, clutching the blade as hard as she could.

At the same time, more delvers poured toward them.

Thomas clapped his watch closed, dropping it to dangle at his side. Sound flooded the scene of the battle, sudden as an unexpected thunderclap. But now the noise was all wild and chaotic. The delver chant was done, the little monsters too absorbed in the fight to continue their evil chorus.

Thomas pulled another watch from his pocket, swung it around his head, and lashed at the delvers with it. Wherever it struck, Cara could hear the hiss of burning flesh. Jacques shouted wildly from behind her.

Before she could turn, he came handspringing past her, into the midst of the delvers. He landed on his feet and began slashing about him with a short blade while the delvers stabbed at him with their spears.

All this Cara saw in a flash. Then her attention was all on her own fight, for the delvers were after her as well. She continued to slash out with the blade M'Gama had given her, wishing as she did that she knew something, *anything*, about how to use it properly. Even so, she was able to keep the monsters at bay, and severely wound more than one of them.

It was not enough. Soon a delver grabbed her from behind, pulling her arms back with a fierce yank. Her shoulders bursting with pain, she cried out and dropped her blade. That didn't stop her from also kicking out, and the delver in front of her fell with a surprised cry.

With a snarl, her captor tightened his grip on her arms. He swung her around.

Cara cried out in astonishment.

CHAPTER TEN

NEW ARRIVALS

Racing out of the forest, exploding into the battle, came Lightfoot. Not far behind the unicorn, slower but plowing ahead like a living tank, was the shaggy, bear-like form of the Dimblethum.

The unexpected attack from a new flank started the delvers shrieking and wailing. The Dimblethum, roaring with rage, flung the little creatures about like rag dolls. Lightfoot snatched one from Belle's back with his teeth and sent it crashing into a tree. Then he spun about and with a powerful kick from his hind legs sent another sprawling into a bush.

In the moment of surprise, Cara wrenched herself free from the delver who held her. Flinging herself to the ground, she snatched up her sword and rolled over just in time to stab upward at a delver who was about to grab her. She pierced his shoulder. He staggered back with a screech of pain.

She was on her feet at once, ready to slash about her. But the battle was over, ended as quickly as it had begun. Clearly overpowered, the delvers chose to retreat, vanishing into the darkness so quickly it was as if the ground itself had swallowed them.

For a moment, no one spoke. The first to move was Cara. Racing to Lightfoot, she flung her arms about his neck. Though Firethroat's gift of tongues made it possible for Cara to speak to anyone in Luster, with Lightfoot she preferred to speak mind to mind.

"I've missed you so much!" she thought. "Thank you for coming!"

Before he could reply, Belle spoke aloud. "I *told* you someone has been following us!"

Moonheart nodded. "So you did. Would you care to explain why that was, nephew?" His voice was stern, disapproving.

"You might thank him first!" said Cara sharply. "He did just save our lives."

Moonheart looked startled, then angry. But finally

he said, somewhat grudgingly, "The child has a point. Our thanks. Now, answer my question."

"I was following you because I was concerned about Cara."

"You want me to believe that *you* have a sense of responsibility?" asked Moonheart scornfully. "You, who have defied your family and refused your place at court?"

"Believe what you want," said Lightfoot, tossing his head so that his mane rippled like a wave.

"And what of *him?*" asked Belle, pointing her horn toward the Dimblethum. "What's he doing here?"

The hulking creature, who seemed to be equal parts bear and man, stood a few feet behind Lightfoot. He clenched his shaggy fists and wrinkled his short muzzle when Belle asked her question, but said nothing.

"We travel together," said Lightfoot simply.

Belle made a sound of disgust.

Now the Dimblethum did speak. "The Dimblethum, too, cares for the child," he growled. But the words were in his own guttural language, and Cara could see that Belle and Moonheart did not understand them.

"Might I suggest we save our arguments for later?" said Finder gently. "It might be wiser to tend our wounds first. Once that's done, we can tear each other up again if we wish."

Lightfoot actually laughed, and the Dimblethum gave a rumbling chuckle. Moonheart scowled, but said softly, "You are correct, Finder. Let's take stock."

It was bad, but not as bad as they might have feared. Thomas and Jacques each had three or four stab wounds, the Dimblethum one deep cut on his side. The wounds were mostly low because the delvers were so short.

"Probably have to amputate," said Jacques, looking at his legs gloomily. "Both of them," he added, though the wound on his left leg was little more than a scratch.

Actually, of the humans it was Thomas who was most severely wounded, his right shoulder cut so deeply that his arm hung useless at his side.

Cara, consumed with worry about her friends, was surprised to find she had a serious wound of her own — a ragged bite mark on her left hand. She had been so involved in the fight she hadn't even noticed it when it had happened.

The Squijum had escaped injury altogether.

The unicorns had taken the worst of it. Cara found it heartbreaking to see the way their crimson and silver blood stained their silken hides. It was mixed with delver gore, which was a muddy green color and smelled of the earth. Finder was badly hurt, though he insisted his wounds were nothing and that he would help with the healing. To Cara's surprise, Moonheart had fared even worse. His flanks were scored with a dozen deep cuts, and bite marks peppered his neck.

"The delvers knew him for the leader, and so attacked him the most viciously," explained Thomas in a whisper as Cara bound his shoulder with a strip of cloth she had cut from her own shirt.

The four of them — Cara, Thomas, Jacques, and the Dimblethum — were sitting under a tree, watching the unicorns examine one another. Though clearly pained by the wounds on his legs, Jacques had been far more concerned about Cara's well-being than his own. Now, finally convinced that she was all right, he was massaging his thigh while he waited for one of the unicorns to heal him. His forehead was beaded with sweat, and Cara could tell he was trying not to cry out.

As she watched the unicorns, she realized that while

she still did not feel comfortable with Moonheart, there was little doubt she owed him her life. Though when it came right down to it, she probably owed her life to each of them. In fact, remembering the cry the delvers had set up when they first attacked, she was certain that must be so.

"Thomas," she said softly. "Did you hear what the delvers were shouting when they attacked?"

"Delvers," growled the Dimblethum in disgust. "Dimblethum crush delvers."

Thomas smiled, then winced as if even that small act was painful. Leaning his head back against the tree, he said softly, "They were crying, 'Get her!' "

Cara's stomach tightened. "Were they talking about me?"

The answer came from Jacques, who said gloomily, "It's possible they were after Belle. She's known to be one of the Queen's fiercest warriors, and the delvers probably have little love for her. But . . . I'd say it's more likely it was indeed you they wanted."

Cara shuddered. "Why?"

"I can see two possibilities, neither good. The first is that they know you are carrying one of the Queen's amulets and they want it. The second, which I like even less, is that they have found out who you really are and have some reason to want *you*. Perhaps they are even in contact with Beloved, though I'm not certain how that could be."

"Jacques is right," said Finder, who had limped over to join their conversation. "We're going to have to be more careful than ever how we travel."

Belle's sharp ears overheard them. "They never should have gotten the jump on us to begin with," she said from where she stood. "I should have been paying closer attention. But my thoughts were distracted by trying to figure out who was following us, not who might be waiting ahead."

"No point in blaming Lightfoot for what's happened," said Finder gently.

"Oh, go ahead," said Lightfoot, glancing at Belle. "You might as well blame me. I'm used to it."

Belle snorted in disgust. Ignoring her glare, Lightfoot turned to Thomas. "Moonheart asked me to tend your wounds. I'll take care of that bite on your hand, too, Cara. But Thomas first, because he's lost the most blood. Finder will take care of the Dimblethum. And Belle will see to Jacques."

Cara knew that in doing all this healing, the uni-

119

corns were at the same time weakening themselves and would need to rest for a while to recover.

"Are you going to fix each other, too?" she asked Lightfoot when he came to tend her hand.

"We'll take care of the worst of the damage," he told her as he knelt beside her and pressed his horn to the place where the delver had bitten her.

She started to answer, but her words were choked by the flash of pain that accompanied the healing. She caught her breath, then bit her lip to keep from crying out. In a moment it was over. She looked at her hand. Though the open wound had closed smoothly, the flesh was still red and angry looking.

"An incomplete cure," murmured Lightfoot. "Delver bites are nasty, and I am at less than full strength. Thomas's wounds were even worse than they looked, and took a lot of energy to fix."

Cara noticed that his legs were trembling. A moment later he sank to the ground beside her.

She had learned the first time Lightfoot had healed one of her wounds — a wound also caused by a delver attack — that the process was extremely draining for the unicorns. She guessed that was why they were going to heal only the worst of each other's wounds. It was probably a kind of balancing act, determining which would slow them down the least: the wounds themselves, or the period of rest required after a major healing.

Putting her hand on Lightfoot's neck, she thought, "I am so glad you've come back. I missed you."

"And I missed you," he replied, his thoughts muzzy with exhaustion.

An instant later he was asleep.

They stayed at the site of the battle for the next two days, keeping watch for the return of the delvers and letting the unicorns regain their strength. Cara fretted at the delay. Rubbing her thumb across the notches on her calendar stick, she counted the days over and over, as if by counting them enough she could somehow change the math of the sky and add to the time they had left before the first day of autumn.

She did take advantage of the delay to spend some time with the Dimblethum, whom she felt she had slighted the day before by rushing straight to Lightfoot.

"I am so glad you are with us," she said to him. "I missed you very much."

"And I missed you, little Wanderer," he replied in his deep, rumbling voice.

The name startled her, and she didn't say much after that. The Dimblethum wasn't one for talking anyway. But it felt good, and safe, to sit beside him. Later, he disappeared for several hours. When she asked Lightfoot about it, he said, "I think he's off looking for delvers to crunch."

Toward the end of the second afternoon, Jacques invited her to take a walk with him. It felt good to be up and moving, even if they weren't really going anywhere. They found a stream about a hundred yards from their resting place. Following it, they came to a large pool.

"Don't go too far," warned Jacques when she waded in to wash. "You'll drown yourself for certain."

She laughed and rolled her eyes, which caused his face to grow even gloomier than usual.

Later they led the unicorns to the pool, and Cara helped them clean away the blood and gore that had covered them after the battle.

"Do you know one of the biggest differences between unicorns and humans?" asked Finder, standing knee-deep in the cold water.

"What?" asked Cara, trying to keep her stomach from turning as she used a handful of *tarka* leaves to scour the filth from his coat.

"Hands," said the big unicorn. "I can never be sure if I'm glad we don't have them, or not. They're plenty useful — certainly it would be easier for us to clean up now if we had them. On the other hoof, they lead you into all sorts of mischief."

Cara held her hands in front of her, spread her fingers, wiggled them. Though she sometimes wished she had been born a unicorn instead of a human, she wasn't sure she would be willing to give up her hands for the privilege.

She returned to her task. "There," she said at last. "Perfectly clean!"

Finder climbed out of the pond and shook his head. His mane spattered water in all directions, like a spray of diamonds.

That night Cara carved the seventh notch in her calendar. "Twenty-four days left," she murmured.

The next morning they began to travel again. Moonheart was still limping a little, but his wounds were healing faster than Cara would have expected.

I wonder if their healing powers work naturally on their own wounds? she thought as she watched him walk. She studied the scar on Finder's shoulder and, by the end of the day, was surprised to see that it had grown significantly lighter.

The Dimblethum dropped behind several times. Lightfoot told her it was because he was covering their trail and devising various methods to confuse the delvers.

Continuing upstream along the river, they emerged at midday from the woods to an open plain. Though the land was flat and open here, it was often marshy, and trying to find a solid path sometimes slowed their progress so much that Cara would grow nearly frantic with worry.

On the far side of the plain rose some low, rolling hills, which they reached toward dusk of the second day. By this time the unicorns seemed to have completely recovered from their wounds. It was just as well, for their path led directly into the hills, where it was not always easy to follow the river. It had sliced deep into the land, and the banks were often steep and high.

To make things more difficult, it began to rain — a

slow, steady drizzle that persisted all through the night and the next day as well.

On the morning of the fourth day after they had resumed their journey, the soggy, grumpy travelers were walking along a rocky wall when they were startled by a rumbling sound.

Looking to her right, Cara gasped. One of the boulders was rising into the air, revealing a dark hole.

From the darkness came a voice, both cranky and familiar.

"Well," it snapped. "It's about time you got here!"

CHAPTER ELEVEN

UNDERGROUND JOURNEY

A small man stepped out of the darkness. His skin was a beautiful deep brown. His eyes, so large they looked almost comic in his serious face, were topped by bushy sprouts of silvery hair. He wore a coarsely woven robe in which shades of red, brown, and orange mixed to make it look rather like a distant view of a forest floor in autumn.

"Grimwold!" cried Cara in delight. "What are you doing here?"

"Well, you were coming to see me, weren't you?" asked the little man, sounding impatient.

"I wasn't sure. I hoped we might, but —"

He cut her off with a wave of his hand. "The Queen sent a message."

"You mean other unicorns have gotten here ahead of us?" asked Cara in surprise.

"Did I say that?" asked Grimwold, rolling his eyes.

"Then how —" She broke off as she remembered the scrying pool with which they had once tried to contact the Queen.

"Arabella has many ways to communicate with me," said Grimwold. "Anyway, she'd heard from M'Gama that you were coming this way and asked me to meet you." He narrowed his eyes. "She didn't mention that there would be so many of you."

"We had unexpected company," said Moonheart sourly.

Grimwold sighed heavily, as if accepting some tragic turn of fate. "Well, I suppose you'll *all* be wanting to come in. Nothing to do about it, I guess. It's not like anyone would really care if it was an imposition, or if I already had more work than I could handle, or anything like that. Come on, come on! We can't stand here all night!"

With that, he disappeared back into the darkness. Thomas began folding up his cart, something Cara always enjoyed watching. It was astonishing to see the huge thing disappear into itself — though she could never figure out exactly how it happened. The Tinker had reduced the cart to something he could easily tuck under one arm when Moonheart motioned for Cara to lead the way.

As she stepped into the dark opening, the Squijum leaped onto her shoulder to ride with her. "Wowza, wowza!" he chattered. "Cranky, cranky old guy!"

"Shhh!" she cautioned. Not because his words weren't true. She just didn't want him to make the situation worse.

As soon as they entered the hillside, she saw a glimmer of light to her right. The passageway turned, then turned again. Rounding the second corner, Cara found herself in a small chamber lined with dark, reddish wood. From the wall hung a lantern, casting a cheery glow. Beneath it stood Grimwold, his hands resting on what looked like the captain's wheel of an old-fashioned ship. On the floor beside him was a backpack.

"You'd better go on a bit," he said gruffly. "Won't be room in here for everyone."

Cara nodded and did as he asked, moving along the stony corridor that stretched to his left. She could hear the others enter behind her, the unicorns muttering in annoyance because the turns were so tight it was hard for them to maneuver.

Finally she heard Lightfoot say, "That's it. I'm the last."

Grimwold grunted. "Are you sure? I was beginning to think the Queen had sent an entire army." He paused, then said, more softly, and clearly surprised, "By Bellenmore's Belt, it's Lightfoot. What are *you* doing here?" He chuckled. "I notice you waited till last to come in. Staying as far from your uncle as you can?"

"I thought you didn't like idle chatter," said Lightfoot sharply.

"Information gathering is never idle."

"Why not just close the door before someone else tries to get in?" snapped Lightfoot.

"What do you think I'm doing?" said Grimwold, sounding equally testy.

Cara heard a *creak*. Looking back past the others, she was able — just barely — to see Grimwold turning the wooden wheel. Next came a rumbling noise, and then a heavy *thud* as the boulder that masked the entry into the hill fell back in place.

A moment later Grimwold joined her at the front of

the procession. He was carrying the lantern that had hung in the small chamber.

"I knew we would be passing near the edge of your territory," said Cara. "But I didn't realize we were so close to it already."

"You're not."

"I don't understand. If we're not near your home, then why are we —"

"This tunnel leads to my home. But it would take us at least a day's journey to get there. Anyway, that's not where we're going."

"I still don't understand," said Cara, beginning to feel frustrated.

"You want to get to the Northern Forest, right?"

"Yes."

"Well, it will take you forever the way you were going. I have a better route."

"All underground?" asked Cara nervously.

"I like being underground. Besides, we'll travel more quickly this way. Making the same trip overland, with all those hills and valleys and forests and other nonsense — not to mention the way that foolish river twists and turns — would take at least twice as long."

Cara felt a surge of relief. Anything that would get them to Ebillan's cave faster was welcome to her.

"You'll probably be safer this way, too," added Grimwold, somewhat as an afterthought.

"That would be nice," said Jacques, who was walking behind them. "I'd just as soon avoid danger as much as possible."

"Sensible," said Grimwold. "Hardly what I would have expected from one of you Players."

Moonheart snorted in amusement.

It was a wondrous journey. They traveled along corridors lined with wood, and others made of stone. Some of the stone passages appeared to have been made by hand; others were obviously natural, sometimes widening so that the entire company could walk side by side. At other times a passage would narrow so sharply that even going single file they could barely squeeze through it. Once they had to stop because the Dimblethum got stuck and howled pitifully until they could free him — which was only possible because Jacques was still behind him, and so could push, while Thomas pulled him from in front.

Moonheart and Belle stood watching this, both looking exasperated.

Shortly after they had freed the Dimblethum, the passage opened into an enormous cave, so big that the light from Grimwold's lantern couldn't penetrate its depths. Ahead of them was a reddish glow. Cara heard a low rumbling sound. As they drew closer to the glow, she could see that it came from a wide gap in the cavern floor.

"How are we going to get over that?" she asked nervously.

Without saying a word, Grimwold pointed to the right, where a narrow stretch of rock spanned the chasm.

"I thought you said this was safer than traveling aboveground," grumbled Jacques.

"I said safer, not risk-free. Besides, if you don't fall off, it's no problem at all."

"I'd rather take my chances in a good, clean fight," muttered Belle.

The rumble grew louder as they walked. From the red glow ahead of them, Cara expected to find the chasm filled with bubbling lava. She was astonished when they reached it to see that the noise was actually made by an enormous cataract — a thundering torrent of water that gushed from a sheer wall about a quarter of a mile to the right, then tumbled fifty or sixty feet to form a river that raged and rolled beneath them and on to their left for as far as she could see.

What made it even more remarkable was that the water exploding from the wall glowed a brilliant red. The spray and mist it threw up were crimson as well, and the river that roared beneath them might as well have been made of blood.

Cara stared at the water in awe. "What makes it glow?" she asked, shouting to be heard above the roar of the water.

Grimwold shrugged. "Could be minerals it picks up as it travels underground. Could be some kind of tiny plant or animal."

"Could be magic," added Thomas.

"Possible," agreed Grimwold, "though if it is, I don't see the point of it."

"Do all wonders need to have a purpose?" responded Thomas.

Grimwold snorted in response, then said, "Follow me." He stepped onto the stone bridge, which was about three feet wide, with an irregular surface. Fortunately it was far enough from the falls that the spray didn't reach it, so the surface was not made slick by water. Unfortunately, the drop to the river below was well over a hundred feet.

"Well, at least it will be a quick death if I fall," said Jacques as he stepped onto the bridge.

Cara followed him, and after a few steps made the mistake of looking down at the glowing torrent. She felt herself sway and had to close her eyes for a moment. After that she forced herself to focus on her feet and not the abyss below.

The Squijum, however, scampered around fear-lessly — shooting ahead, zipping back and forth across the bridge, even climbing over the edge and clinging to the side. Cara tried to ignore him until he got under-neath her feet and nearly tripped her. "Squijum!" she snapped. "Get up here on my shoulder before you kill me. And don't move until we get to the other side!"

"Hotcha stinky cranky girl," he muttered sullenly. But he did as she told him.

They stopped at the top of the bridge's arc to admire the waterfall. Turning to her left, Cara could now see that the river flowed in a straight line for another mile or two, then disappeared out of sight — though whether it plunged over another falls, or the cavern ended and the river simply began flowing through a tunnel again, she could not tell.

Once across the bridge it took another hour to reach the far side of the cavern. Cara had no idea how Grimwold kept on track, for there was no path that she could see, and the space was so large that even the echoes of their footsteps seemed distant. But that he did keep on track there was no doubt, for when they finally came to the far side, they were directly in front of a small tunnel, no more than five feet high and three feet wide. It was tiny compared to the vastness of the cavern wall, and if you missed it you could have spent hours, maybe days, trying to find it — and that was assuming it was the only one and you didn't go wandering off in the wrong tunnel altogether.

"How did you bring us directly to this spot?" asked Cara.

"Practice," grunted Grimwold as he entered the tunnel.

Another hour or so of traveling brought the group to a comfortably sized cave that was dimly lit by glowing, pale blue fungus that grew on rocks surrounding a pool of water.

"We'll stop here for the night," said Grimwold.

"How do you know it's night?" asked Jacques.

The old dwarf snorted. "I listen to my body. Do you have to have the light to tell you everything?"

Jacques shrugged. "If I listened to *my* body, it would be time to rest all day long."

Thomas pulled out one of his watches, opened the top, shook it once, then said, "It's night all right."

Grimwold snorted. Setting down his pack, he opened it and removed a large knife. He began slicing chunks of the blue fungus away from the rock — chunks that he distributed to the others.

"You want me to eat this?" asked Cara in dismay.

"You can wear it if you'd rather. I suspect, however, it will do you more good inside than out."

She took a tiny bite. This was Luster, after all. Maybe it would turn out to be unexpectedly delicious.

It didn't.

"Yuk! Ptooie!" sputtered the Squijum, who had tried a bit at the same time. "Nasty, nasty, nasty!"

My sentiments exactly! thought Cara as the Squijum spat the fungus onto the rock where he was crouching.

To her surprise, the others seemed to think it tasted just fine. She wondered if it was one of those weird foods that only grown-ups seem to like. Sheer hunger forced her to take two more bites. Then she gave up.

Now that they had stopped moving, she could feel the coolness of the caves. She took the cloak M'Gama had given her from her pack and wrapped it around her shoulders. She also took out her calendar stick and carved another notch.

Eleven days gone. Would they make it on time, or not?

Despite her worries over the time, despite her hunger and the hard stone floor, exhaustion worked its magic, and she was soon fast asleep.

They spent most of the next day traveling in single file through narrow tunnels, which made it difficult to speak to the person ahead of you — especially if the person ahead of you was a unicorn. And the few times they came out into the caverns, the vast spaces seemed somehow inappropriate for talking, as if the huge underground rooms had a sacred quality.

When they did enter the more open areas, Cara made it a point to take turns walking beside each of her companions. She spent the most time beside Lightfoot and the Dimblethum, of course. But she wanted all of them to know they were important to her, that she cared for them.

It hurt her heart that Moonheart and Belle were so obvious about avoiding the two newest members of their band, always positioning themselves as far from Lightfoot and the Dimblethum as they could and refusing to speak to them unless necessary.

She wished they could all be more friendly with each other.

Dinner was better that night, for they came to a cave with an underground stream and the Dimblethum was able to catch some fish for them. Pale and blind, with enormous, sightless eyes, they were ugly to look at but extremely tasty.

At least, tasty for raw fish, thought Cara, finding herself actually thankful that her grandmother had insisted she try all kinds of food over the years, up to and including sushi.

When they had finished eating, Grimwold called them together and said, "Tomorrow I will be sending you back to the world above. So tonight I want to share a story with you."

Cara was surprised to hear a whicker of satisfaction from Belle, who then added, "It would have been quite a thing to travel three days with the Keeper of the Chronicles and not be given a story."

"I give you this one at the request of the Queen."

"What story is it?" asked Cara, excited but also a little nervous.

Grimwold looked directly at her.

"It is the tale of how your grandmother first came to Luster. When you're ready, I'll begin."

CHAPTER TWELVE

IVY'S STORY

Cara glanced around the cave, which was lit only by Grimwold's lantern. Despite the lack of comfort, despite the chill, despite her exhaustion, she felt an odd sense of happiness. These . . .

She faltered in her thoughts. What to call this group? Not "people" — that word wasn't big enough to properly include the unicorns, the Dimblethum, and the Squijum. And "creatures" seemed too — well, animalistic, or something. Maybe "beings" was the right word.

No. Not beings.

Friends.

She felt surrounded by friends. The journey was long and hard, but traveling together had forged them into a kind of family of the road that was filling a need in her heart.

Moonheart, Belle, and Finder had settled themselves in a group to Grimwold's right. Thomas had opened his wagon, which looked particularly strange here inside the cavern, and he and Jacques were sitting on the tailgate. The Dimblethum lounged nearby, growling gently as he picked at the last bits of the fish, while the Squijum was splashing cheerfully in and out of the water. And Lightfoot — her dear Lightfoot — had taken his place beside her. Wrapped snugly in her cloak, she leaned against him to listen.

While the travelers had been trying to make themselves comfortable, Grimwold had opened his pack and taken out a large, leather-bound book, into which several brightly colored ribbons had been inserted as page markers. He waited until everyone was quiet, then said, "When Queen Arabella contacted me through the scrying pool and asked me to help Cara on her journey to the Northern Forest, she also requested that I tell Cara this story." He looked directly at her. "I was well prepared to do so. I had started digging into the Chronicles after the last time I saw you, looking up some stories I had recorded many tens of years ago — stories about your grandmother."

He settled the book in his lap and placed his lantern

on a boulder next to him. Looking at Cara again, he asked, in unusually gentle tones, "How much do you know of your grandmother's past?"

Cara glanced at Jacques, feeling a little embarrassed. "Not much," she said at last.

Grimwold nodded. "Then I'll start at the beginning." He opened the book to a page marked by a scarlet ribbon. "This is Ivy's story — the first part of it, at least. She told it to me herself many years ago. She was a young woman then, and these are her own words, exactly as she spoke them."

I remember almost nothing of my early years. According to Mr. Preston, the director of the orphanage where I lived, I had been found wandering in the hills outside of the town. It was a small town in England, near the border with Wales.

When they brought me to the orphanage, I appeared to be seven or eight years old. Though I could speak clearly and well, I did not know my name or where I had come from.

Eventually Mr. Preston named me Ivy. He said he chose this name because sometimes I would sit and stare out the window for hours on end, gazing at the forest and the mountains that rose behind it, as if I were rooted to the spot. But other times I would wander off, going much farther than I should, so that people were frantic to find me. "Ivy has roots, and yet it rambles wherever it can," he said. "Just like you."

Except I didn't have roots, not really; how could I, when I had no memory of family or home?

The first images I can bring to mind are of my room in the orphanage. The room was small, and I shared it with three other girls. They often teased me because of my strange ways, and sometimes I would cry because of this. But just as often they were friendly, and I have more good feelings about them than bad. And while I longed for a family, the orphanage was not really a bad place. I was cared for, fed and sheltered, and had friends to play with.

One day Mr. Preston called me into his office and said, "Ivy, I have someone here I would like you to meet."

Sitting in the small sofa was a short, cozy-looking woman who looked like she would be nice to hug. Next to her sat a tall man, lean and hard looking. He had reddish-brown hair, dark eyes, and a hawk-like nose. He smiled. It was a warm smile, friendly and inviting. For some reason, I found it terrifying.

"This is Mr. and Mrs. Martin Hunter," said Mr. Preston. "They're interested in adopting you."

I took a step back.

Mr. Preston laughed. "Don't be silly, Ivy. You want a home, don't you?"

I wanted a home more deeply than he could imagine. The very word created a longing so intense, it was almost painful. But not with these people. I didn't know why. I only knew they terrified me.

I shook my head.

Mr. Preston laughed again, but it was a shorter, harsher sound than the first time. "Don't be silly, Ivy. You know that we can't keep you on here if someone is willing to take you in. You should be pleased. Mr. and Mrs. Hunter have been watching for a long time, and out of all our orphans they've chosen you."

I shook my head again, mute with a horror that I could not explain.

"Oh, she'll come around soon enough," said Mrs. Hunter with a laugh. The sound was warm and gentle, as cozy as she looked, and I felt myself thawing toward her. But it did nothing to lessen my dread of her husband.

Mr. Preston dismissed me. While I was out of the room, the deed was done. Later that afternoon Mr. Preston called me back to his room, scolded me for my behavior earlier in the day, and told me that next week I was to go live with the Hunters.

"And you'd best be grateful for this, Miss Ivy," he said sharply. "Be grateful and act proper. I don't want you showing up on our doorstep again because you're not willing to be civil to these pleasant folk who are willing to take you in. I've been glad to have you here, strange poppet that you are. But our goal is to find you a home, and now that you have one, you'd best take advantage of it."

That night, I resolved to run away.

Two nights later, I did. Rising after dark, I tip-

toed from my room without waking the other girls. In the kitchen I took a loaf of bread, some fruit, and some cheese — not enough, I now realize, to feed me for more than two or three days. But I was less worried about how I would eat than whether anyone would catch me.

I slipped out through a window that I knew had a broken latch, planning to head for an abandoned cottage I had discovered during one of my "rambles." I thought I'd stay there, at least for the next day or so until the Hunters went away.

I had not traveled far from the orphanage when I heard footsteps behind me. I froze in terror, but only for a moment. Moving quietly, with a stealth I had not known that I possessed, I slipped into the bushes at the side of the road.

It was not long after that I saw a man come riding by. Though he was a tall man, he was leaning low over his horse's neck. He glanced from side to side, and in the moonlight I could see his face.

It was Martin Hunter.

The night was cool, but the chill I felt when I saw him came from something deeper, a terror that I could not explain.

He rode on, but it was a long time before I dared to move again.

It was nearly dawn before I made it to the cottage. Though it was cold, and the floor itself was made of earth, my exhaustion was such that I slept for hours.

For two days I was left in peace. I wandered the forest and felt both a happiness and a terrible longing that I could not understand. Then, late in the afternoon of the second day, I heard footsteps through the trees.

Fearing it was Mr. Hunter coming to get me, I fled, going deeper into the woods, toward the mountains.

I moved silently at first, until I was a good distance from the hut. Then I ran as fast as I could, ran until my side felt as if it had been sliced open and my lungs burned as if I were breathing fire. Just when I thought I was safe, I heard someone behind me again. I stumbled forward, nearly blind with exhaustion — and stepped into emptiness. I remember the terror of falling. Then, for a time, there was nothing.

When I came to my senses it was dark, and I was in tremendous pain. My leg, especially, hurt; when I tried to move it I quickly realized I had broken it. I wanted to scream but didn't dare for fear Martin Hunter might still be looking for me; though I didn't know why he was chasing me, I was certain I didn't want to be caught.

The night seemed endless. I drifted in and out of an agony-filled daze, trembling so violently from pain and shock that I feared I would crack my teeth. It wasn't until morning that I saw I had fallen over a cliff. The bushes had saved my life — perhaps saved it twice: first by cushioning my fall, then by hiding me from the man who was after me, though whether he realized I had gone over the cliff, whether he had found a way down to look for me, I had no way of knowing.

Every moment hurt. I vomited from the pain. Yet I couldn't stay where I was. It took several hours, and I blacked out several times during the process, but I managed to drag myself out of the bushes.

I was in a narrow valley, bordered on both sides by cliffs some thirty or forty feet high. I could hear a stream gurgling through the center of the valley, so I pulled myself in that direction, both because I was so parched I could hardly swallow and because I figured if I had any chance of getting help, of being found, it would be near the water.

But, truthfully, I did not expect anyone to find me. I expected to die there.

I had thought about death many times, wondered what it was like, what it would mean. Yet somehow I had never quite believed it would happen to me.

Now I did.

By the time I dragged myself to the stream, my leg felt as if someone had hammered nails straight through the bone and now was trying to pull them out again. I plunged my face into the icy water and drank, then rolled over and blacked out again.

When I woke, the sky — what I could see of it, for much was blocked by the cliffs — was a deeper black than I had ever experienced. The stars, in turn, were more brilliant than I had imagined possible. I gazed up in awe, so startled I nearly forgot my pain in that first moment.

It reminded me soon enough that it was there.

I grabbed a low branch of a nearby shrub and clenched it in my hands, trying to keep from crying out. I wanted to be found, but not by anything that might have been prowling through that darkness.

My silence did me no good. I was found, anyway, and a good thing for me that I was.

Grimwold paused and looked up. The listeners were silent, even the Squijum, who had curled himself up on Cara's lap. She stroked his gray fur, wondering why her grandmother had never told her these things.

Glancing around at the others, she was startled to see that Moonheart looked troubled, as if he was deeply bothered by the story.

"Shall I go on?" asked Grimwold.

"Of course," Cara would have said, save that the question was clearly directed to Moonheart.

The others glanced in his direction.

After a moment he nodded and said, "Continue."

What was that all about? wondered Cara. But she didn't have time to ponder it, for the story had begun again.

He came so quietly [read Grimwold] *that I had no idea he was approaching. When I first saw him, so white in the starlight, his shape blurred by my teary eyes, I thought perhaps it was the moon. But as he came closer, I realized I was being approached by a unicorn — which made me think I had died, or gone mad. So I was only a little terrified when, once he was close enough, he bent his head and pierced my chest with the tip of his horn, driving it toward my heart.*

For a moment I felt as if my skin had turned to light, as if my blood had become electricity. Then the strange tingling passed; with it went much of my other pain as well.

"Alas, poor maiden in the woods," said the unicorn. "I am sorry to frighten you. But I needed to do that so we could communicate."

To my astonishment, he spoke not in words but in pure meaning — meaning that came from images, sounds, memories, even smells that formed directly inside my head. "Where did you come from?" I asked eagerly. "How did you find me?"

"Don't speak aloud! I can't understand if you

do. Just form the thought and send it to me. You'll have to stay in contact with me to do it."

I didn't want to lose contact with him, not now, not ever. Gripping his foreleg with my hand, I thought again, "Where did you come from?"

"Earth, originally. Now, from another world."

I found the strangeness of these words nearly as frightening as any of the other things that had happened to me.

"How did you get here?" I asked. "Are you lost? Are you scared?"

"I came through a gate. I came because you needed me."

This was so startling I broke my contact with him for a moment, dropping my grip on his foreleg as if it had burned me. He nickered softly, and I placed my hand on his leg once more. It was smoother, silkier, than anything I had ever felt.

"How did you know I needed you?" I asked.

He paused, and when he finally answered, I could sense a deep pain in his words. "We unicorns have long had a connection to young maidens in the woods."

"There are more of you?" I asked eagerly, for I

had heard the legend that there is never more than one unicorn on Earth at a time — not that I had believed there were any at all until I saw this one.

"Not here," he said, sounding as lost and lonely as I felt. "Not here." Before I could ask another question, he said, "I can heal you if you would like."

"Please!"

He had me stretch out flat on the ground, and then examined me. Finally he said, "I am going to ask you to do something difficult."

"What?"

He gestured with his horn toward a nearby shrub. "Wedge your foot in those branches, then pull yourself back until the leg is straight again. It will hurt like fire. But the leg is badly broken, and I can heal it better if the two parts of the bone are more in line. Do you think you can do that?"

"Of course," I said, trying to sound braver than I felt.

And I did, though the searing pain made me scream.

The flash of agony when he healed me was even worse. But that was over in an instant. I sat up.

To my astonishment the leg was solid and whole once more. The pain, though not completely gone, had faded to a shadow of what it had been.

"Now I must rest," the unicorn said. He started to kneel, but his legs buckled before he could get all the way down, and he collapsed beside me. I pressed myself against him, trying to keep him warm. But in truth it was his presence that kept me warm through the night.

In the morning I was able to walk, which felt better than I would have imagined.

"We must get away from here," said my unicorn. He led me along the ravine, then into another, then up an isolated mountain to a craggy area where he showed me a hidden cave. Once we were inside, I could tell he felt calmer, more relaxed.

"Now we must talk," he said.

"About what?" I asked.

Before he could answer, a man leaped out of the darkness. I recognized him at once. It was Martin Hunter.

"This is for Beloved!" he screamed.

Then he plunged his sword into the unicorn's side.

CHAPTER THIRTEEN

THE JEWEL

Grimwold paused in his story, rubbed the back of his hand over his brow, then glanced at Moonheart, almost as if seeking permission to continue.

But it was Cara who urged him on. "What happened next?" she asked eagerly. She was fascinated by this secret history of her grandmother. Yet at the same time, the intrusion of another Hunter into the story left her once more horrified by the chain of family that tied her to the vengeful Beloved. She would have given her life to protect the unicorns, and she couldn't help feeling vaguely guilty whenever she thought of her father's side of the family.

"Give me a moment," said Grimwold. He went to

the stream from which they had taken the fish, dipped in his hand, took a drink of water.

Then he returned to his place and, by the light of his lantern, began once again reading Ivy's words:

The unicorn reared back. Silver and scarlet blood pumped down his silken coat as he pawed the air with his hooves, trumpeting in pain and fury.

The man slashed out with the sword again. As he did, I flung myself at him, grabbing his arm. Startled, he turned toward me, raising his hand to strike me. But the unicorn struck first, his hooves thudding against the man's head.

Our attacker cried out, then crumpled to the cave floor.

My unicorn stood for a moment, blood pulsing from his side. Then he, too, collapsed.

I threw myself down beside him, put my hand on his neck. I was sobbing, but forced myself to stop. "Are you all right?" I thought, realizing it was a stupid question even as I asked it. "What can I do for you?"

"Get help," he thought, and the message as it came to me was red and swirling with pain. "Get help."

"How?"

"Back of the cave . . . another cave . . . find gate."

"A gate?" I asked, feeling confused. Why would there be a gate in a cave?

"Gate to . . . Luster. Find . . . other unicorns. Tell them . . . Moonheart needs help."

Cara gasped. *"Moonheart?"*

"I never knew about this!" said Lightfoot, sounding equally surprised — and slightly amused.

"There is a great deal you don't know, nephew," said Moonheart severely. "Continue with your story, Grimwold."

The old dwarf nodded and began to read again.

At first, I was not willing to leave my unicorn, my Moonheart. But I could do him no good where I was. So I made my way to the back of the cave. I traveled a little distance in darkness, through a narrow passage. Then I saw a light ahead of me. Turning a corner, I entered another cave, larger than the first. I stopped short, gazing in awe at the most amazing thing I had ever seen.

The gate — it had to be the gate — floated in the center of the cave, its base a foot or so above the floor. It was a perfect circle, twelve feet high at least, with a surface that shimmered like water and glowed with the tender green of springtime. I was delighted — and terrified. I walked up to it nervously, then pressed my hand against the surface. I felt a pleasant tingling. I pressed harder, and my hand went through. At once the tingling flowed along my arm.

I cried out and pulled my hand back. Then I walked around to the other side of the circle. It looked exactly the same as the front. Standing at the edge of the circle so I could see both sides — it was no thicker than a penny — I thrust my hand forward again.

To my astonishment, though my hand went in, it didn't come out on the other side!

I pulled my hand out, gasping with fear, and was relieved to find it still attached to my arm.

What was on the other side of the circle? Not the other side here in the cave — I had seen that. What happened if you went through *the gate, as I was supposed to do?*

I wanted to run away. But Moonheart was counting on me.

I began counting myself, intending to step through the circle at three, at five, at ten, but hesitating each time. "I'll do it when I get to twelve," I promised myself, starting again with one.

And I did. When I reached twelve, I plunged through the circle — and into the world that would claim half my heart for all my life.

Though I had crossed from a cave, I stepped out onto a mountainside. Though I had crossed from morning, I stepped out into twilight.

In a circle of trees a little way below me stood a glory of unicorns — though I didn't know, then, that "glory" was the proper term for a group of these wonderful creatures. I stumbled toward them, awed by their beauty, terrified that they might run. I needed them, needed them desperately, to come help Moonheart.

To my relief, they remained standing, watching

*me. After a moment I gained control of myself.
Slowly, holding one hand before me, I approached
them as you would a skittish animal. I didn't
know, then, how foolish that made me seem; didn't
know that I was the skittish animal.*

*They held still, let me come to them. I placed
my hand on the neck of the one closest to me.*

"Moonheart needs help," I thought desperately.

*"He wants us to come to the other side?" he
replied. I could sense the horror in his response, feel
it in my stomach as if it were my own.*

*"Yes. A man attacked him. He's been stabbed.
He's bleeding. I'm afraid he might . . . might die."*

*The unicorn's anger, surging into me through
our connection, almost knocked me over. I staggered away, losing my contact with him. He spoke
to the other three unicorns, and they raced up the
hill. Leaping into the glowing circle, they disappeared from sight.*

And that was how I first came to Luster.

Grimwold closed the book.
"That's it?" demanded Cara.

"That's the story the Queen asked me to tell you," he replied with some asperity. "The tale of how your grandmother came to be here. I assume she had her reasons for wanting you to know it."

"But what happened next?"

"I survived," said Moonheart dryly.

"What were you doing on Earth to begin with?" asked Lightfoot.

Moonheart closed his eyes. "I was having a Wander Year. A year, mind you," he said emphatically, opening his eyes and looking directly at Lightfoot, "not an eternity. I wanted to see the Seven Gates, both to satisfy my curiosity and because I knew I would someday be charged with the care and guardianship of them. That was a responsibility I took seriously."

The Squijum, distracted by something, bounded off Cara's lap and scurried into the darkness.

Moonheart snorted and continued his story. "The glory that was guarding the fourth gate welcomed me — until I told them that I could sense something wrong on the other side, could sense a maiden in the woods who needed help.

"'That's no business of ours,' said the leader —

Silkmane was her name — 'we stay in Luster, where we belong.'

"I knew she was right. But all through the night, Ivy's feeling of need, of terror, of pain, continued growing in me. Finally I went to Traveler, who was standing the late watch, and said, 'I am too restless to sleep. I'll take your place for a while.' He was only too happy to agree, and went contentedly off to stand drowsing with the others.

"I waited, biding my time, until I felt certain none were alert. Then I bolted through the gate."

"*You* went against orders?" snorted Lightfoot in astonishment.

Cara, her hand on Lightfoot's flank, thought, *Hush! He'll never finish the story if you embarrass him!*

Moonheart looked uncomfortable, but ignored the question. "It didn't take me long to find her. But there was a mystery then, and it remains now: Why was I able to sense Ivy's need when none of the others could? Why was I able to sense that need all the way from the other side of a gate? What made that need so compelling that I was willing to abandon common sense, to flout the rules, in order to respond? That is not the way of things as we know them. That is not *my* way."

He turned his head so that he was speaking directly to Lightfoot. "And yet, I have never regretted what I did. After all, it brought Ivy Morris to live among us. And when my Wander Year was over, I did the right thing and went back to court."

His voice held a hint of accusation, aimed directly at Lightfoot, and something sharp and angry seemed to float in the air between them.

Cara, uncomfortable, said, "I still want to know what happened next."

"The others found and healed me," said Moonheart.

"And what of the Hunter?" asked Cara, knowing that she must be in some way related to him, as she was to all the Hunters. With a shudder she realized he might even have been her grandfather on her father's side.

"He woke as the others were healing me. When he saw so many of us together, he tried to flee. But we couldn't let him go, now that he had found the gate — couldn't let him take that information back to the others."

"You didn't . . . kill him, did you?" asked Cara.

"He would have killed me," said Moonheart coldly.

"But no, we didn't kill him. We brought him back here and put him in the hands of a person who deals with such things for us. She put him to sleep, rather like the princess in your 'Sleeping Beauty' story."

"And he's still sleeping?" asked Cara in astonishment.

"Do you have a better idea for dealing with him?" snorted Belle.

"No. I just . . . no."

"Actually, there are times I almost wish to wake him," said Moonheart, "for there are questions I would still like answered. Our feeling is that the reason he wanted to take Ivy from the orphanage was to use her as a lure for a unicorn, in the way that Hunters have always placed young maidens in the woods. Yet the Guardian of Memory was thousands of miles from that place, so there was no unicorn for him to catch until I arrived. Why set a trap where there is no unicorn? Hunters are not fools about these things. It was almost as if he knew I would be coming. But though Beloved and her Hunters have many skills, reading the future has never been one of them. So how could he have known? And why was it Ivy, in particular, who he wanted — wanted so much that he tried to track her down when she fled? He could have taken some other girl from the orphanage if all he wanted was a maiden to lure a unicorn."

Moonheart shook his head, causing his mane to ripple over his neck. In the glow of Grimwold's lantern it looked like liquid light. "I have pondered these questions many times but have not been able to make sense of them. And yet, I do not regret what happened, for it brought Ivy to my side, and that was a great joy. She traveled with me for the rest of my Wander Year, and we had many adventures together. When the year was over she was offered a home at court with the Queen. She turned it down, which was a bit of a scandal. But it was as if there was something in her that could not bear to be at rest. She was always looking, seeking. Sometimes I wondered if because I was a Wanderer myself when we first met that she had been somehow infected by my own restlessness. But I think it was more than that. Alas, whatever it was that made her a Wanderer was one mystery she kept to herself."

"Indeed," said Grimwold, and Cara had the sense that he was deeply annoyed at not knowing the whole story.

"There's nothing wrong with wandering," said Finder quietly.

"No, there's not," agreed Moonheart, "not if that's what you're born to do. But with Ivy there was always a sense that she was not merely wandering, but that she was looking for something — something she could not even name."

"Or perhaps that some secret sorrow kept her in motion," said Jacques, who had been silent to this point. "I sometimes felt that she feared if she stayed in one place too long, some old pain or loss that she could not speak of, perhaps couldn't even really remember, would rise up and devour her."

"There are things even a unicorn can't heal," said Moonheart sadly.

I wonder if Gramma's wandering had anything to do with losing her parents? thought Cara.

"Eventually your grandmother became a messenger for the Queen," said Grimwold. "Which is not a bad job for someone who is a wanderer by nature. She was one of the few to travel regularly back and forth between the two worlds. She has more adventures recorded in the Chronicles than I can count."

"She was using the amulet all that time?" asked Cara, putting her hand to her neck.

Grimwold shook his head. "No, the amulet was given to her at the end, when she decided to return to Earth for good. She had done the Queen a great service then, and no one wanted her to go. But she insisted. The amulet was so she could return to Luster when she wanted. It has a particular quality in that regard. While I know it dropped you in the wilderness when you first arrived, its magic was tuned in such a way as to bring the Wanderer back to the Queen, wherever she might be."

"Yet she didn't come back," whispered Jacques, his face still and solemn, its lines deep with age and loss. "I don't know why."

"She used to sing about her wandering," said Grimwold. Then, to Cara's surprise, he began to sing "Song of the Wanderer" himself. After a moment, Jacques joined him, their voices blending in an unexpectedly lovely harmony.

It was a long song, filled with a need so deep it was like the sound of a heart being torn in two.

Across the gently rolling hills,
Beyond high mountain peaks,

SONG OF THE WANDERER

Along the shores of distant seas,
There's something my heart seeks.

But there's no peace in wandering,
The road's not made for rest.
And footsore fools will never know
What home might suit them best.

But, oh, the things that I have seen,
The secret paths I've trod,
The hidden corners of the world
Known to none but me and God.

Yes, the world was meant for knowing,
And feet were meant to roam.
But one who's always going
Will never find a home.

Oh, where's the thread that binds me,
The voice that calls me back?
Where's the love that finds me —
And what's the root I lack?

And between each verse the now familiar chorus:

> *My heart seeks the hearth,*
> *My feet seek the road.*
> *A soul so divided*
> *Is a terrible load.*
>
> *My heart longs to rest,*
> *My feet yearn to roam.*
> *Shall I wander the world*
> *Or stay safe at home?*

"That was her final gift to us," said Jacques when they were done. "That —" He broke off. Pointing to Cara's finger, he cried, "What does *that* mean?"

Cara glanced down. M'Gama's ring was glowing, as it had the first night she'd heard Jacques sing the song.

"I don't know," she whispered. She held up her hand. The green light of the ring, almost dazzling in its intensity, began to fade even as they all stared at it.

"Where did you get that?" asked Grimwold gruffly.

"M'Gama gave it to me," said Cara, still staring at her hand even though the ring had lost its light.

"She always was one for a touch of mystery," muttered Grimwold. "As for gifts — a song and a ring are all fine, but odds are good you are going to need yet another gift before this is over, if the message I got from the Queen is correct. She said you were heading for Ebillan's territory?"

The Dimblethum growled at the mention of the name.

"Yes, well, that's very impressive," said Grimwold, nodding at the manbear. "But it will take more than growls to convince that dragon to let you pass in peace."

"Do you have any suggestions?" asked Cara.

"He is fierce and unpredictable," said Grimwold. "The best way to reach him is through his greed."

"Alas," said Finder, "we have nothing to bargain with."

Grimwold smiled. Reaching into his robe, he drew forth a scarlet gem the size of a duck egg. "This may be of use," he said, sounding just a trifle smug.

He extended it to Cara.

"Are you sure you want to give this up?" she asked, awestruck by the size and beauty of the jewel.

"What am I going to do with it?" he asked scornfully. "Eat it? I don't want to throw it away on a fool's errand. But if you can make good use of it — if it will help you bring back the Wanderer — then take it."

Hesitantly, Cara accepted the jewel from his hand. It looked like fire and felt like ice. Staring into it, she felt herself being lost in its crimson depths, wandering among its facets, almost as if she had entered another world. Forests of red, rivers of red, towering mountains and deep caverns, all blazing red, rolled out before her.

As she walked along the scarlet paths, one tree in particular seemed to call her. Unaware now of Grimwold, of her friends, of anything save the jewel, Cara let her mind drift forward.

The tree had a big hollow at its base.

Cara stooped to peer into it.

Inside sat a woman dressed in a white robe — the only white Cara had seen in this red world. The woman had her hands clasped before her and her head bowed so that her long red hair covered her face.

Suddenly she snapped her head back, flinging her hair behind her. Cara gasped at the beautiful face revealed by this gesture. The wide-set blue eyes, the high cheekbones, the full lips were all achingly familiar to her, familiar for a simple reason: They belonged to her mother.

CHAPTER FOURTEEN

THE WILDLANDS

For a moment Cara couldn't move, couldn't speak, was afraid, indeed, that her heart would stop beating. Finally she whispered, "Mommy?"

Her mother, whom she had not seen since she was three, stared at her for a long time without answering.

"Don't you know me?" asked Cara, her voice quavering.

Suddenly her mother's eyes grew wide with astonishment. "*Cara?* Cara, is that you?"

"Yes! Yes, it's me, Mom. What are you doing here?"

Her mother looked around. Then, her voice troubled, she said softly, "I don't know. I don't know at all! Where am I, Cara? *Where am I?*"

"How did you get here?" Cara asked urgently. She stepped forward, reaching toward her mother. But the moment she touched her, the vision was over. It ended not with a flash of light, nor a roar of thunder. Her mother's image simply vanished, and Cara found herself once more in Grimwold's cave, staring at the scarlet jewel that lay in her trembling hand.

She took a deep, gasping breath. When she looked up, the others could see tears trembling in her eyes.

"What just happened?" she whispered.

"What do you mean?" asked Jacques. He was bending over her, his leathery face wrinkled with concern.

"What just happened?" repeated Cara, a note of wildness creeping into her voice.

Moonheart stepped forward. "You were staring into the jewel — studying it as if you were reading something hard to understand. Just as I was starting to wonder if something was wrong you cried out and shook your head."

"I was here all that time?" she asked, still trying to catch her breath.

"Where else would you have been?" asked Grimwold, his voice unusually gentle.

Closing her fingers over the jewel — holding it as tightly as if it were her own heart, trying to escape — she told them what had happened.

Jacques was the first to speak, the first to break the silence that followed her story. "What does it mean?" he asked. His voice was ragged, almost desperate, and Cara suddenly realized that if he was indeed her grandfather, then her mother would be his daughter — a daughter he had never seen.

Grimwold shook his head. "I have no idea." He sounded disturbed, even frightened.

Cara loosened her grip on the jewel. Feeling foolish, yet knowing she had to ask, she pointed at it and said, "Is it possible. . . could my mother be *inside* this thing?"

"I hesitate to say anything is *impossible,*" said Grimwold. "But I doubt that is the case. More likely the jewel offered a focal point for you to connect to your mother — possibly because it is connected to whatever magic holds her."

"But there are other possibilities, too," said Thomas. Cara turned to him. "Like what?"

He took a watch from one of his pockets, consulted it, and returned it to a different pocket, jingling his chains as he did. "One is that you simply imagined the whole scene, saw it because you want your mother so much."

Cara started to object, but he raised his hand.

"Another is that the jewel itself carries an enchantment, one that makes you see things that are unsettled in your life. It could be a positive enchantment, forcing you to face issues you haven't dealt with. It could be a negative one, meant to torment you and lead you into false action."

"Why would someone cast a spell like that?" asked Cara, appalled at the thought and resisting the idea that she had not actually seen her mother.

Thomas shrugged. "The ways of magic users are strange and mysterious. But it doesn't even have to have been a purposeful spell. It might be some natural property of the jewel, or some side effect of it having been kept in a place where magic was in use. But there is one more possibility to consider: What if the message is false?"

"What do you mean?"

"Remember back in Summerhaven, when you dreamed of Beloved? I suspect that dream came because Beloved was trying to reach you — though I'm not sure *why* she was able to do it then."

"What are you talking about?" demanded Grimwold.

Quickly, Cara told him the details of the horrible experience she had had the night before they left Summerhaven.

"The Tinker is right," said Grimwold. "This may well come from Beloved. If it does, she was probably using the jewel as a focus point to reach you. But if so, what was the focus point the first time? And why hasn't she tried again until now? That's something I'd dearly like to know."

"But why would Beloved send me a vision of my mother?" asked Cara desperately.

"It could be designed to throw you off balance, or turn you from your path," said Thomas gently.

Cara felt as if she would choke on the confusion and despair swirling in her breast. "How can I know for sure?"

"There *is* no way to know right now," said Grimwold. "That is why such messages are usually of so little use, and may even be dangerous. They can lead you into journeys you were not meant to take, turn you toward paths you were not meant to follow. For now, simply hold the vision in your heart. Later, you may learn something that will help you understand it — and understand what to do about it."

She opened her fingers. The jewel lay in her palm, flashing scarlet and crimson in the torchlight.

"Should I look in it again?" she asked fearfully.

"Not now," said Grimwold, closing her fingers back over it.

"You had better keep it," she said, thrusting it back toward Grimwold. "I could never give it to Ebillan, not after what just happened. You'll have to give me something else to use."

"Do you think I keep things like this just lying about?" demanded Grimwold indignantly. "Bits of treasure to cough up on demand?"

Cara blushed as she realized that Grimwold had freely given her something worth a fortune to help her on her quest, and that now she was demanding he take it back and give her something different. "I'm sorry," she murmured. "But I don't know what to do with it."

"Do whatever you want," said Grimwold gruffly. "I've given what help I can. I need some rest now. I'd suggest that you lot do the same. Tomorrow I'll lead you to the best place to reenter the world above."

When everyone had settled for the night, Grimwold extinguished his lantern.

The blackness of the cave was utter, and complete.

Even so, and though she knew she should rest, Cara could not get to sleep. Despite her exhaustion, the story of her grandmother's entrance into Luster, and even more the strange episode with the crimson jewel, continued to circle in her mind.

She could not decide which was more complete: the darkness of the cave, or the darkness inside her.

The next day Grimwold led them through a series of tunnels, then up a long slope that brought them out onto the side of a low mountain.

"This is as close as I can take you to your destination," he said. "The River Silver is that way. I wish you well on the rest of your journey."

He turned away, and Cara thought that was all he was going to say. But after a moment he turned back, turned to face her specifically. "When you find the Wanderer, give her my greetings. Tell her . . . tell her she owes me a story." He turned once more, and vanished into the darkness. A moment later a boulder slid silently into place, blocking the entrance.

"Come," said Moonheart. "We'd best get moving."

◆　◆　◆

It was Finder who took the lead now, picking his way skillfully down the mountainside so that even the humans could travel without too much slipping and sliding. They heard strange cries as they walked, and more than once the sound of something slithering away from them. Cara realized with a start that there were probably hundreds — maybe thousands — of kinds of animals here that she was totally unaware of. If the ones she had seen so far were any indication, they would be like the ones she knew on Earth, and yet somehow . . . different.

They reached the Silver before noon. The river was considerably smaller here, closer to its source. They followed it north for the rest of the day. Late in the afternoon, they came to a flat stretch of grassland. On the far side of the grassland, rising like a wall, just as M'Gama had described it, was the Northern Forest.

It was nightfall by the time they reached the edge of the forest, and they made their camp at the corner formed by the river and the forest.

Cara took out her calendar stick and carved the day's notch. Thirteen days. Grimwold's shortcut had brought them here ahead of schedule.

Her heart felt lighter than it had in days.

◆　◆　◆

The next morning they traveled east along the forest's edge. About noon they came to the black stones that M'Gama had described. They were unmistakable — smooth, about three feet in diameter, and towering to ten feet in height. They stood about five feet apart, and Cara shivered as they walked between them.

But the path was there, just as M'Gama had promised, true and straight.

As darkness began to fall, they found a resting place at the base of an enormous tree. Its bark, remarkably smooth for such a big tree, was silvery-blue. The trunk was so big that Cara, Jacques, and Thomas together could not reach their arms around it. Its massive roots rippled the ground for yards in all directions, creating long, low mounds, sometimes heaving right out of the soil so that their tops looked like long, silver snakes stretching out from the tree. Cara made a pile of leaves between two of these roots, and in this way created a cozy bed for herself.

The next day the territory they entered was wilder still. Cresting one hill, Cara noticed an area off to her right that seemed oddly out of focus. At first she thought it was due to a light mist that hung over the area. But as she kept staring at it, that didn't seem right. When she drew Finder's attention to it, he said, "No one has explored that area yet."

"But why does it look that way?" she persisted.

"Because no one has explored it yet," he repeated.

"What does exploring a place have to do with how it looks?"

"I'd rather not talk about it," answered Finder. His discomfort only increased Cara's curiosity. But when she tried another question he made it clear that he wouldn't say any more on the topic.

The going was more treacherous now — the hills steeper, the forest thicker and denser. Once, the path led them into a swamp, where they nearly lost the Dimblethum when he stumbled into murky water that began to suck him down as if trying to swallow him. His roars of distress were deafening, and for the first time Cara saw fear in the great creature's eyes. Jacques and Thomas struggled desperately to pull him out, but it was only when Cara and the Squijum found some vines that they were able to use as ropes that they managed to get him free of the clinging muck. His shaggy coat was thick with slime, and though he longed to wash it off, he was afraid to enter the water again. It was not until late the next day, when they found a clear stream, that he managed to get clean.

Three nights later they made camp beside another stream. As usual, Thomas and Jacques placed themselves on either side of her, each about four feet away. She knew they did this so that she would feel safe, and she appreciated it. The Squijum curled up at her feet, then on her chest, then beside her head, then disappeared for a while, then came back to lie beside her again. She was vaguely aware of his restlessness as she drifted on the edge of sleep, but not bothered by it since he was that way most of the time. The unicorns, who needed less sleep than the others, stood to one side, talking softly among themselves.

All around them were the sounds of the night — the breeze that moved softly through the leaves above them, the shrill chirp and singing of the insects, the flick of wings from creatures that flew only in the dark. In the distance something howled mournfully at the moon. Cara rolled over, and the leaves rustled beneath her. To her right a shelf of fungus attached to the trunk of a large tree glowed pale blue.

The night wore on. The sounds began to fade. Yet Cara could not sleep. Finally she sat up. Rummaging in her pack, she found the jewel Grimwold had given her. Moving as silently as possible, she got to her feet. She stood for a moment, uncertain what to do.

I need more light, she thought.

But M'Gama had warned them against leaving the path.

I won't go far, she promised herself. *Certainly not out of sight of the camp.*

Looking around, she found a spot only a few yards away, where the trees were not blocking the moonlight. She crossed to it, trying to move as quietly as if she were a unicorn herself. Once in the light, she held up the jewel and stared into it, waiting to see her mother again.

CHAPTER FIFTEEN

MOANS IN THE DARKNESS

Nothing happened.

Cara stared harder, holding her breath, willing the magic to work once more.

Nothing.

Angry and frustrated, she resisted an urge to fling the jewel into the darkness. Forcing herself to breathe deeply, she gazed up at the black velvet sky. The stars were flung across it in wild abandon, jewels themselves, winking with distant fire. She sought out the few constellations she had learned so far: the Queen, the Guardian, the Snake, the Ravager.

Her eyes lingered on the Ravager, and as they did she found herself drifting into a waking dream once more. She felt a moment of fear when it began. Then, thinking she might see her mother again after all, she released herself to it.

She was in a cave lit by torches. The torches indicated a path, and she followed it, drifting as if her feet did not touch the floor. Down she went, deeper and deeper into the cave, into the dream. She came at last to a great wooden door. She touched it with her fingertips, and it swung silently open.

On the far side, where she had hoped to find her mother, she saw instead Beloved.

The woman gestured to her. Unable to resist, caught as if in a spell, Cara took a step toward her.

"Welcome, daughter of my daughters," whispered Beloved. Her eyes were warm, her tone soft and caressing. "Come closer."

Telling herself she shouldn't, longing to hold still, Cara took another step forward.

"Closer," whispered Beloved.

Cara was trembling now. But she took another step.

Beloved reached out to embrace her.

"Where is my mother?" asked Cara. "Do you know?"

"Of course I do. Give me the amulet, and she is yours."

Cara longed to obey. She felt her hand going to her neck. With a ferocious effort, she stopped herself. *No!* she thought. *No, I won't!*

"Give it," whispered Beloved eagerly.

Feeling as if her heart were splitting, Cara lifted the amulet from her shirt. She gazed down at it. Her fingers shook as she touched it once again. With a sudden cry, she turned and ran, out of the cave, and out of the dream.

Awake, Cara found herself standing in the moonlight once more, in the night of Luster, just outside the circle of her friends. But the terror had seized her, and without thinking she ran into the forest, slipping and stumbling as she did, running as if she could leave her life, the tangled web of her family, far behind.

She charged on until the air burned in her lungs and her side throbbed with pain. When her legs could no longer hold her, she tripped over a root and fell crashing to the ground.

She lay there for a time, gasping and sobbing. Finally she rolled over and looked up.

Now she was seized by a new terror. *What have I done?* she thought, furious with herself for letting her fear drive her away from her friends.

Suddenly, M'Gama's warning about not leaving the path echoed in her ears.

"How could I have been so stupid?" she cried.

Immediately she regretted speaking aloud, and wondered if there was anyone nearby to hear.

She pushed herself to her feet, looking desperately for some sign of the way that she had come. But the forest was deep here, and neither starlight nor moonlight could penetrate the leaves. The darkness was complete.

She was lost in the wildlands of Luster.

She stumbled forward, her hands outstretched as if she were blind, until she came to a tree. She wrapped her arms around it, clung to it as if to a life raft that would support her in the sea of darkness that surrounded her.

She had scarcely caught her breath when a new terror shook her. For out of the deep and surrounding darkness came a low, shuddering moan.

Cara tightened her grip on the tree. As the first jolt of fear subsided, she began groping above her, searching for branches she could use to pull herself up, away from the ground.

She heard the moan once more. It was still frightening. But it didn't sound angry, and — more importantly — it didn't sound any closer than it had before. So whatever it was, it wasn't coming after her, as she had feared.

She tried to slow her breath, to make herself as still and silent as possible.

A light breeze stirred around her, rustling the leaves with its coolness. She began to edge around the tree, hoping to put it between herself and the source of the moans. After a step or two, she turned around, realizing it would be better to have her back to the tree and be facing out so she could detect any approaching danger — though what good that would do in the forest darkness she wasn't sure.

When Cara reached the far side of the tree, she slid to the ground and curled herself into a small, miserable ball. Her flight into darkness, being lost, the strange moans in the night, and, most of all, the vision of Beloved — it was all more than she could take.

As she huddled there, trying not to cry, she heard

the moan once more. It was low and sorrowful —
sounding, in fact, much like she felt. It roused a kind
of pity in her, and she began to wonder if she should
go in search of the sound to see if she could offer some
help.

Don't be stupid! she told herself. *Stay right here until
sunrise. If the moaning is still going on when it gets light,
then you can go look.*

But her heart wouldn't listen to her mind, and as the
next moan came shuddering out of the night, she
found herself forgetting her own problems and wondering what would cause anyone to make such a
mournful sound.

For a long time after that she heard nothing. The
sudden silence frightened her almost as much as the
moaning had.

What if whoever it was has died? she fretted. She lay
in an agony of indecision, unwilling to venture into the
darkness, knowing she couldn't see to find anyone anyway, and yet still feeling she ought to do something.

After what seemed like hours, she heard another
moan. She was almost relieved. Pulling herself to her
feet, she started toward the sound. She moved slowly,

both because she could not see, and because she wanted to remain silent in case whoever was making the sound was dangerous after all.

She stumbled twice within the first few steps she took and realized that getting to her feet had been a bad idea. She dropped back to her hands and knees. Putting her right hand ahead of her, she swung it from side to side, then lowered it gently to the ground, trying not to snap any twigs or rustle any leaves as she did. Then she moved her right knee forward as well.

She repeated the process with her left hand and knee.

Her progress was excruciatingly slow. But then, she was in no particular hurry, her concern about whoever was moaning being nearly balanced by her fear.

Wings fluttered overhead, and she wondered what kind of animals flew at night in this forest. In the distance she heard a howl — like a wolf's, but lower and deeper.

Realizing again how little she knew of Luster and its wildlife, she shuddered. But she also continued her forward motion.

Suddenly, as if announced by the howl, the moon appeared. Though its silver-blue light was mostly blocked by the forest above, her eyes were now so dark-accustomed that even these shreds of light allowed her to move much more easily.

Another moan told her she was off course. She adjusted to the left and continued forward.

A few feet more brought her to a large boulder — so big that as she worked her way along it, she thought at first it was a cliff. But soon enough she felt it curve, and could see by the faint dapple of moonlight that it was only a stone after all.

Now she moved more cautiously than ever. Even so, when she put her hand down onto a thick stack of feathers, she shrieked and scurried backward.

At the same time, a harsh voice cried, "Gaaahhh! Don't kill me!"

Cara pressed herself against the rock, trying not to betray her position by so much as a breath.

After a moment of silence, the voice cried, "Well, if you *are* going to kill me, stop fooling around and let's get it over with, gadfound you."

"I don't want to kill you," said Cara softly. She felt braver now, thinking that anything so afraid of getting killed was unlikely to be out to hurt *her*.

"Then what are you doing here?" asked the voice suspiciously.

"I heard you moaning and came to see what was wrong."

"I was *not* moaning!"

This remark startled Cara so much that she said, "If it wasn't you, then who was it?"

"I don't know. But Medafil does not moan." The voice hesitated a second, then added, "Besides, wouldn't you moan if you were trapped, and had probably broken a wing, and you figured the delvers were going to come and kill you at any moment?"

"Yes," said Cara. "I would. Definitely."

"Well, there you go," said Medafil. "It wasn't me. But it would have been all right if it had been."

"How are you trapped?" asked Cara.

"Why don't you come around and see?" asked the voice wearily.

"How do I know you won't eat *me* if I do?"

"What would I want to do that for?" replied the voice, sounding shocked beyond belief.

"Because you're hungry?"

"Gaaaah! If I wanted to eat you I would have come

around that dadgimbled rock and done it by now. At least, I would have if I could move."

This didn't entirely make sense to Cara, but she pushed herself to her feet anyway. Still somewhat wary, she stepped a few feet away from the rock before she continued around it.

What she saw in the dim moonlight filled her with wonder, terror, and pity.

CHAPTER SIXTEEN

MEDAFIL

The creature was magnificent, even in distress. His head was that of an eagle, or would have been if not for the tufted ears that rose from its sides. His wings, too, could have been those of an eagle, except that they were vastly bigger than any eagle's had ever been. But there the resemblance to an eagle ended. From the shoulders down, Medafil's body was that of a great, tawny lion — though twice the size of any normal lion.

"A gryphon!" Cara whispered in awe. "You're a gryphon!"

"Well, what's so surprising about that?" the creature snapped. "You're a girl. Very unusual around here. Even so, you don't see me lying here with my mouth hanging open, gawping at you about it."

194

"But I've never seen a gryphon before."

"How old are you?"

"Twelve."

"Well, it's been longer than that since I've seen a girl. So who's the more surprised, eh? Now, if you want something really surprising, consider the fact that a gryphon let itself be trapped like this. Gaaaah! It's . . . humiliating."

Looking more carefully, straining to see in the dim light, Cara realized that the gryphon's right front leg was caught by a thick snare. Walking cautiously to him — she wanted to trust him but she also knew that his beak could take off one of her own legs with a single snap — she knelt to examine the snare.

It was made of many strands of wire, woven together to form a cable as thick as her thumb. One end of it was anchored under the boulder, though how that had been done, she couldn't imagine. The other formed a loop around the gryphon's leg that had been pulled so tight it nearly disappeared beneath his fur. That the fur was wet with blood testified to his struggles to break free.

"Who would have done this?" she asked, horrified and outraged all at once.

"Delvers," replied the gryphon, his voice filled with disgust. "Who else?"

"But why?"

Medafil shrugged one of his wings, creating a small breeze. "Why do birds fly? That's the way they are."

"How did they capture you?" asked Cara, trying to work her fingers into the wire loop to see if she could loosen it.

"I'd rather not say," replied the gryphon. He sounded embarrassed. But before Cara could press the point, he added, "Oh, all right, I'll tell you. They cheated. They played on my weak point."

"What's that?" she asked, still working at the wire.

The gryphon clicked his beak in annoyance. "I like shiny things. I collect them. Old family habit. Can't help myself. The delvers have lots of shiny things, of course. Bladratted creatures rooting around in the ground the way that they do are always coming across gold and jewels. So they made this."

"What?" asked Cara.

"This," he said impatiently, moving his front leg. She gasped. Hidden beneath his enormous paw had been a gem-encrusted sphere that would have been worth a fortune back on Earth. "They left it out here for me to find, knowing I wouldn't be able to resist it. And they set that snare to catch me when I went after it."

"I would have thought they'd have been watching to see when you got caught," said Cara, glancing around nervously. "Why haven't they come to get you yet?"

"They're in no hurry. The trap may have been here for weeks already. They probably check it every other night or so."

"Weren't they afraid that someone would steal the . . . the bait?"

"Well, anyone who tried would have been trapped just like me. Besides, who else would there be to take it?"

Given the fact that they were in a deep, nearly unin-habited wilderness, Cara could think of no answer for that question.

Turning back to the snare, she said, "I think I'd better go look for the others. I don't think I can do this by myself."

"Gaaaahhh! Don't go. If the delvers come while you're gone, they'll kill me. Gadbingled things will probably eat me, too. Very undignified way for a gryphon to die."

Cara didn't want to face the delvers again herself. Even the idea made her shudder. But she couldn't leave the creature here to face them on his own. So she began working at the wire snare again. For a time it seemed that the more she worked, the tighter it got. Once the gryphon hissed in pain and stretched his great beak toward her as if he was about to bite her. When she gasped, he stopped and drew his head back, blinking a bit and looking ashamed. She made no comment.

I wish I hadn't left my sword behind when I ran off, she thought as the wire began to shred her fingertips. Her blood was matting in the gryphon's fur, mingling with his own.

The unicorns can heal the cuts, she kept telling herself, mostly as a way to try to ignore the throbbing pain.

Finally deciding that she was not going to be able to loosen the snare, she groped around until she found a sharp rock and began to saw at the wire.

"Gaaah!" cried Medafil. "You're cutting me!"

"Well, I've already cut myself!" she snapped, growing impatient with the creature. "Do you have a better idea?"

"Gramding it," he muttered, which she took to mean, "No."

At first she thought the rock would be no more effective than her fingers had been. But finally she felt a strand of the wire snap. Another went, and then another. It took a full ten minutes, but finally she had severed the entire cluster of wires.

As soon as she was done the gryphon surged to his feet, shrieked with triumph, and flapped his wings. Dust and twigs blew all around her.

"Well," said Cara dryly. "I guess your wing isn't broken after all."

"I couldn't tell at first," sniffed Medafil. Tucking his wings against his sides, he sat, much the way a cat does.

Cara had to look up to see his face. His eagle eyes blinked down at her, and the sharp blade of his beak made her nervous.

"What are you doing here, anyway?" he asked.

Cara started to reply, but realized she wasn't sure how much she should say about her mission. She had begun to realize there was more going on in Luster than she had first thought. "I'm looking for someone," she replied evasively.

Medafil scowled at her. "Are you a friend of the Queen or not?"

Cara felt herself relax a bit. The clear implication was that only a friend of the Queen would be welcome here. "Friend," she said happily.

"And who are the 'others' you mentioned earlier?"

"I'm traveling with a band of unicorns."

"Then what are you doing out here on your own? Don't you know the danger of leaving the path in *this* forest?"

"I had a . . . a vision. It frightened me, and I ran away. That was pretty stupid, I suppose. But I wasn't thinking straight. About the time I realized I was lost, I heard you moaning —"

"I wasn't moaning," said Medafil sharply. Then, letting his wings sag, he said, "Oh, all right, I was moaning. A little. And you're not going to forget it, are you? Think you have a hook in me now, don't you?"

"Why are you so suspicious?" asked Cara.

"I'm not! And never mind anyway. Now, do you want me to take you back to these unicorns of yours?"

"That would be wonderful."

"All right. I owe you that much at least. But there's no point in looking for them until morning. And there's not much point in staying here, either. Why don't we go back to my aerie?"

"I don't know," said Cara nervously.

"Why are you so suspicious?" asked Medafil mockingly. "If I wanted to eat you, I could do it right here."

"Maybe you want to share me with your mate," replied Cara quickly, surprised at her own boldness. "Or maybe you've got a nest full of babies who prefer their food live."

Medafil turned away. "I have no mate," he said bitterly.

The hurt in his voice was so sharp that Cara's suspicion was replaced by pity. "I'm sorry," she said, stepping forward to stroke his side. "I didn't mean to —"

"Never mind," he said sharply. "Climb on my back, and let's get out of here. No, wait. Go get that bauble they used to trick me with. No sense in leaving it around here for the delvers. Unless you're secretly working for them."

"Don't be silly!"

"Well, you can't be too careful," said the gryphon.

Cara picked up the jewel-crusted sphere, then climbed onto Medafil's back.

"Ready?" he asked. Without waiting for her to answer, he began to run, flapping his great wings as he did. She leaned forward to grab his feathered neck.

A moment later they were airborne.

Cara cried out in delight as they rose into the night sky. Medafil circled higher and higher. In the moonlight she could not see the details of the land, only the broad strokes of it — the forest, the mountains, and, in the distance, a glimmering body of water. "What's that?" she called.

"What's what?"

"The water over that way."

Medafil shuddered beneath her. "Gaaah! That's Lake Death. Don't talk about it."

He turned away from the lake, beating his wings harder still. They continued to rise. In the moonlight Cara saw the rocky slope of a mountain. The air was cold and thin, and as they neared the mountain she could see that they had passed above the tree line.

"Home," said Medafil a moment later as he settled onto a rocky ledge. Cara slid from his back onto a surface that was littered with an odd collection of items: clean-picked bones, some tiny, some nearly as long as she was tall; a scattering of shiny baubles, some of which looked quite valuable; and a dozen or so long, tawny feathers that looked very much as if they had come from Medafil himself.

"Sorry," said the gryphon, kicking aside a bone. "Not very tidy. Bachelor quarters, you know. View's good, though."

Following the gesture of his wing, Cara turned to look out on the world below. Vast and unsettled, silvered by moonlight, the beauty of the forest that stretched into the distance was so stark, it made her catch her breath. She stared at it for a time, drinking in the wonder of it, then rubbed her arms. "Cold up here," she said.

"Come inside," said Medafil. "It's warmer."

She followed him into the cave that opened at the back of the ledge. "Don't you have any light?" she complained as she stumbled over more debris.

"Why should I? I can see perfectly well in the dark."

"Well, I can't," she replied testily.

"Well, you don't live here," he snapped back. "But if it means that much to you, I'll see what I can do. Hold still. I'll be right back."

This speech was followed by the sound of him rummaging through the debris on the floor. "Drat!" he muttered. "I know that thing was around here some-where. Ouch! Dingfangled pointy things. No, not that. Grambabbit, where is the spartbongle anyway?"

After several minutes of this, he exclaimed tri-umphantly, "There you are, you splitgiddled thing. Thought you could hide from me, did you? Hah! And hah again! Now shine. Shine!"

Nothing happened.

"Drat!" said the gryphon. "I forgot how to make it work. Here, see if you can do anything with the dim-buggery thing."

He dropped a large sphere into Cara's lap. Smooth and cool to the touch, it was nearly the size of a bowl-ing ball. Fortunately, it weighed scarcely more than a feather.

No sooner had Cara placed her hands on it than the sphere began to glow with a soft light.

"Gaaah!" cried Medafil. "I forgot! It only glows for humans. That's why I never use the spligfitted thing."

"It's beautiful," said Cara in awe. "Like a giant pearl lit from inside."

"Well, you can't have it. So don't even think about trying to steal it."

"For heaven's sake! Why are you so suspicious?"

"It's my job. I'm a treasure guardian. I have to be suspicious."

"Don't you trust anyone?"

"Not hardly. Certainly not humans. No, I take that back. There was a human I trusted once, for a while. Until she broke my heart. A girl like you. Little older, maybe. Hard to tell with you humans. We used to call her the Wanderer."

"She's my grandmother!"

"Gaaah!" cried Medafil angrily. He stood, looking suddenly menacing in the pearly light.

Cara shrank back against the wall.

"She owes me something," said the gryphon, looming over her. "An old debt. I think it's time to collect."

He started toward her.

CHAPTER SEVENTEEN

SHELL AND SPHERE

Cara stood and began backing away from the gryphon, holding the sphere between them like a shield. "What is it?" she stammered. "What does my grandmother owe you?"

"A kiss! She promised. She promised, and then she left without giving it. A cheat, a cheat after all. And I trusted her!"

Cara blinked. "Is that all? Well, come here, then. I'll be glad to kiss you."

"You will?" asked Medafil suspiciously.

"Certainly." She nearly added that she had always kissed the neighbor's cat back at home, but decided against it. She wasn't sure Medafil would like the comparison.

He sat in front of her, wings tucked against his sides, eyes closed, tail curled around his front paws. Cara set the sphere gently on the cave floor. Then she placed her hands on the gryphon's neck. Stretching upward, she kissed him firmly on his beak.

Medafil opened his eyes. "Well, that's better!" he said happily.

"But why did my grandmother leave without kissing you?" Cara asked. "She always keeps her promises."

"Gaaah! I don't want to talk about it! Well, if you must know, we were having an argument. She was stubborn, even for a human." He sighed. "She said she was coming back. But she didn't. She didn't come back."

"I'm going to get her," said Cara gently. "That's why we're out here in the wilderness to begin with."

Medafil blinked in surprise. "What are you talking about?"

So she told him her story, beginning with the night she had jumped from the tower of St. Christopher's and landed in Luster. As she spoke, he stretched on the floor beside her. After a few minutes she heard a deep *thrum* and realized that he was purring. The purring stopped when she described the path M'Gama had told them to follow.

"Ebillan!" he cried, sitting up. "Gaaah! You can't go there. You'll never come back!"

"I have to go."

Medafil let out a heavy breath. "Well, I may be able to help you through the forest. But when it comes to Ebillan, you're going to be on your own. Gaaah, what a terrible idea!"

He stood and began pacing back and forth, his tail twitching as he did. Suddenly he stopped. "I just remembered something that you should have. Something I want to give you."

He went to the back of the cave. After several minutes of listening to him mutter and fuss, Cara picked up the sphere and walked to where Medafil was standing. "I can see why you have a hard time finding anything," she said, gazing at the pile he was pawing through. It was an odd mixture of natural and hand-crafted items — large gems, ancient-looking daggers, lumps of gold, pieces of driftwood, candles, a crown, two shields, and dozens of other things jumbled together in a huge heap.

"Need a housekeeper," muttered Medafil. "Ah, there we go!"

Reaching forward, using his claws delicately, almost like fingers, he extracted a large seashell from the pile. "Here," he said proudly, passing it to Cara.

Shifting the sphere so that she could hold it in one hand, she took the shell. Its outside was a pale, creamy color and rough to the touch. Turning it over she could see that its deep purple throat — smooth and shiny as burnished metal — curved into hidden depths. "It's beautiful," she said. "But why —"

"Hold it to your ear," said Medafil eagerly.

Cara smiled indulgently, figuring the gryphon thought the old trick of "hearing the ocean" in a shell was some special magic. Not wanting to hurt his feelings, she put the shell to her ear, ready to feign surprise.

Her pretend surprise quickly turned to complete astonishment. Though it was indeed the familiar "roar of the ocean" that she heard at first, it soon faded, to be replaced by the voice of a young woman. Though Cara had never heard the voice before, it was oddly familiar.

The words it sang were even more familiar:

My heart seeks the hearth,
My feet seek the road.
A soul so divided
Is a terrible load.

"Where did you get this?" she asked, taking the shell from her ear. She noticed that M'Gama's ring was glowing again, more brightly than ever.

"The Wanderer gave it to me," replied Medafil. "She was supposed to give me a kiss, but she gave me that instead."

"Is that her voice?"

"Of course!" The gryphon looked at her suspiciously. "Don't you recognize her voice?"

"I never heard her voice when she was young," said Cara. "She was much older by the time I was born."

"That makes sense," said Medafil with a nod. "I keep forgetting how quickly you humans age. Anyway, keep the shell. Keep the ball, too, if you like. I don't have much use for it since I can see in the dark. Sort of."

"Thank you," said Cara sincerely. "I don't think I can take the ball, though. It's too big and too fragile. I'm afraid I would break it the first day."

"Oh, nonsense. It's not fragile at all. Watch!"

Reaching forward, the gryphon knocked the glowing sphere out of her hand. Immediately it went black. She heard it hit the stone floor with a bell-like sound, then start to roll away. She could hear Medafil pounce and slam one huge paw down on the sphere, which let out a clear, high note.

"Pick it up," said Medafil.

Groping forward through the darkness, Cara found the gryphon, found his leg, found the sphere. As soon as she picked the ball up, it began to glow again.

"Put one hand on top, the other on the bottom," said Medafil. "That's right. Now twist your hands in opposite directions."

Again, she did as he directed. The sphere began to grow between her hands.

"Oops," said the gryphon. "Try the other way."

She reversed the direction of the twisting. The sphere began to shrink, reducing to the size of a cantaloupe, then a grapefruit, then a tangerine. When it was no bigger than a cherry, she stopped for fear of making it disappear altogether. She held it up for a moment, marveling at its brightness.

"Put it in your pocket," said Medafil.

She did as he instructed. The minute it left her hand the light was extinguished again.

"I'm glad it goes out," she said, "since it would be dangerous if it stayed on all the time. On the other hand, it would be good to be able to let go of it when I'm trying to do something. Is there a way to keep it glowing without holding it?"

"How should I know?" said Medafil, shrugging his wings. "I can't work the gatbangled thing at all! Look, it's getting light. I'd better take you back to your friends before they get worried. Or even worse, before they decide to start looking for you. If they leave the path, we may never be able to find them."

Cara could see just the faintest glimmer of light in the sky at the front of the cave. When she walked toward it and could look out toward the horizon, she saw that fully half the sun was already above the edge of the world.

"You're right!" she said, suddenly terrified that her impulsive action would leave the others thinking something terrible had happened to her — and lead them into danger when they tried to find her. "Let's go. Now!"

"Actually, I'm not sure I want to," said Medafil, sounding sly and stubborn. "Maybe I want you to stay here with me."

"Oh, don't be silly. I have a job to do!"

Medafil sighed. "You sound just like your grandmother."

Cara smiled. "Take me back, and I'll give you another kiss."

"Gaaah! You gave me one kiss because you had to. I don't want another unless you want to give it to me. Come on, let's go."

She mounted his back, and he raced toward the front of the cave. He sprang forward, leaping out over the ledge. When Cara saw the sudden drop beneath them, hundreds of feet down to deadly, jagged rocks, she couldn't help but cry out. But Medafil had spread his great wings and, without even flapping them, he caught an updraft and roared into the sky.

Cara saw Moonheart and the others before they spotted her. When they did look up—it was Finder who spied Medafil first—there was a sudden uproar in the camp. Watching it, Cara could see they feared

213

Medafil was on the attack; Belle and Lightfoot were already moving into battle position.

Leaning against the gryphon's neck, Cara called, "Don't go too low yet. Let me shout to them first."

Holding his wings steady, Medafil glided down to about fifty feet above the travelers, then banked sideways in a curve so they could see Cara mounted on his back.

"It's all right!" she shouted, waving to them. "He's a friend!"

She could see them relax. A moment later, Medafil landed.

"Thank goodness!" cried Jacques as Cara scrambled down from the gryphon's back. "When I woke and found you were gone, I was afraid something terrible had happened."

"Well, something *terrifying* did happen," said Cara.

As she spoke, the Squijum scrambled up her side to perch on her shoulder. "Bad girl!" he scolded. "Gone long scare Squijum bad! Much naughty!" And with that he gave her hair a yank.

"Ouch!" said Cara. "Cut that out."

"Yike! Don't yell!" He gave her a little kiss on the

cheek, then leaped off her shoulder and ran to hide behind Thomas.

When everyone had gathered, she introduced Medafil, then quickly filled them in on all that had happened the night before, starting with her vision of Beloved.

"Hmmmm," said Thomas, taking out one of his watches and glancing at it.

"What?" asked Cara.

"I'm not sure. But there's something familiar about how it happened. I'm trying to figure out what the connection is, what makes this vision like the one you had back in Summerhaven. But I can't put my finger on it."

"We thank you for taking care of our friend," said Moonheart formally, making a slight bow to Medafil.

"Gaaah! She is a friend of the Queen, whom I honor. She is the grandchild of the Wanderer, whom I love. Of course I took care of her. What kind of framdatted care are *you* taking, leading her into Ebillan's territory?"

"It is the path we were given," said Moonheart.

"How are you planning to get there?" insisted the gryphon.

"We'll continue as we are going now," said

Moonheart. "Through the forest and to the edge of his territory."

"You'll never make it unless you follow my advice. Well, you probably won't follow my best advice, which is to not go there at all. But at least let me help you."

"How?"

"The forest is enchanted. Unless you go the right way, you'll wind up wandering in endless circles and never find your way out." He reached back to preen one of his wings with his beak, then said modestly, "I happen to know the paths."

"The only path we need is the one we're on right now," said Moonheart. "If we stay on it, we'll be just fine." These last words he delivered with a significant look at Cara.

"I know a shortcut," said Medafil, sounding almost desperate now.

Cara, ever aware of the calendar stick she carried in her pack, caught her breath. "Moonheart, that might make all the difference," she said softly.

"How do we know he's not simply going to lead us into some trap?" said Moonheart.

Cara, uncertain how to answer, finally said, "We just have to trust him."

Moonheart looked uneasy.

"Trust beak-faced wingcat?" squeaked the Squijum, peeking out from behind the Tinker's boots.

Medafil started to lunge at the little creature but managed to hold himself back.

"Why not trust now?" asked the Dimblethum. "Can always crunch later if need to."

Moonheart sighed. "Lead on," he said.

"I think I'll go home instead," said Medafil.

But Cara put her hand on his shoulder. "Please?"

"Gaah! Dradfingled girlthings. Always could talk me out of common sense. All right, follow me."

And with that, he plunged into the forest.

It took three days to reach the far side of the forest. During that time Cara grew deeply fond of the crotchety gryphon — despite his constant warnings of impending doom. And he more than proved his worth when he twice kept them from being lured onto a false path that would have sent them wandering in the untracked wilderness.

At night, after they had made camp and settled in to rest, Cara followed two rituals. The first was to take out her calendar stick and cut a notch for the day just past.

The notches were growing numerous, the days left for them to reach Ebillan's cave before the transit point would shift again fewer and fewer.

Once she had marked the stick, she would return it to her pack and take out the shell Medafil had given her. Whenever she held it to her ear to listen to her grandmother's voice, M'Gama's ring would begin to glow with a gentle green light. One night Jacques saw her with the shell and asked about it. Without saying anything, she handed it to him. He put it to his ear. After a moment his eyes widened, then filled with tears.

He sat listening to it for a long time.

The Dimblethum was enormously useful in keeping them fed as they traveled, for he seemed to know every plant that could be used in any way for food. Yet he grew fidgety as they continued. When Cara asked him why, he growled, "The Dimblethum does not like dragons. Most especially, he does not like Ebillan."

This did nothing to make her feel any more comfortable.

Cara noticed that Lightfoot often walked alongside Belle. She wanted to ask him about it but wasn't able to maneuver him away from the others until late in the second day. They were walking at the back of the group, Cara with her hand resting on Lightfoot's shoulder. They were silent for a while. Finally, gathering her courage, she said, "Do you like Belle?"

"What do you mean?"

"You know! Do you *like* her? Do you want her to be your girlfriend?"

Lightfoot curled his lip. "The warrior queen for a girlfriend? Now there's a scary thought. Besides," he muttered, "it wouldn't make any difference if I did."

"What do you mean?" asked Cara.

But he shook his head and said, "If we're going to talk, let's talk about something sensible!"

They spent most of the third day after she met Medafil — the twentieth day of their journey — climbing. At the end of the day they came out on a low cliff. Stretching before them was the Northern Waste, a vast, bleak-looking stretch of land, rocky and nearly bare of vegetation. Smoke curled up from cracks in the ground. Ahead, and to the right, Cara could see a muddy pool that popped and bubbled.

"A vacation paradise," muttered Jacques.

"Ebillan's territory," said the gryphon. He reared back and flapped his wings as if he wanted to get away from the land. "This is where I leave you bitdingled fools. Unless you decide to do something intelligent and turn around, too."

Cara looked at Medafil in surprise. Somehow she had assumed he would continue to travel with them. But, of course, he had no connection to their quest and had only come this far as a courtesy.

She went to stand in front of him. "Thank you for your help."

"Gaaah! What have I done but help you to your doom? Dingbongled dragon will probably eat you before you go two miles into his territory. Why not turn around and come back with me?"

"I can't. You know I can't."

"Gaaah," said Medafil. But this time it was little more than a sigh, and his wings sagged as he said it. "I knew you were stubborn from the minute I met you." He looked around, then straightened his shoulders and said, "All right. I was just testing you, hoping you would see the wisdom of turning back. If you insist on going forward, then so be it. Let's get going."

Thus it was that, on the twentieth day of their journey, the Dimblethum, the Squijum, four unicorns, three humans, and one gryphon climbed down the cliff into the Northern Waste that was the territory of Ebillan, the seventh dragon.

To their left the sun was low in the sky. From it stretched brilliant ribbons of red and orange, their garish light making the desolation appear all the more stark. Then, against one of the ribbons of light, Cara saw something else.

"Look," she whispered. "Ebillan. He's coming!"

CHAPTER EIGHTEEN

TO BARGAIN
WITH A DRAGON

Ebillan's body was sinuous, and his long tail writhed and twisted like a snake even as he flew. He was jet-black, save for his eyes, which were a blazing red, and his nostrils, which glowed like hot coals. As he swooped toward them Cara noticed that he was considerably smaller than Firethroat. Even so, each of his bat-like wings was easily as long as a schoolbus.

Suddenly he threw back his head and shot a gout of flame into the darkening purple sky.

Finder stepped back nervously.

"Just a warning," murmured Thomas, and though the words were reassuring, Cara thought he sounded less like he was offering a fact than trying to convince himself that this was the case. She stepped closer to

Lightfoot, who stood tense and ready. Belle was beside him, one foot pawing the stony soil as if she was about to launch herself forward. Moonheart had stepped to the front of the group, where he stood without flinching.

Cupping the air with his wings, Ebillan dropped gracefully to the ground, landing about twenty feet in front of them.

"Yike!" whispered the Squijum, who clung cowering to Cara's neck. The Dimblethum, standing behind her, put one heavy paw on her shoulder.

She glanced over at Medafil. "Gatbimbled thing," muttered the gryphon.

"How dare you enter my territory?" growled Ebillan. His head wove back and forth as he spoke, and his long tongue flicked out of his mouth, nearly lapping against the travelers.

"We come on a mission from the Queen," said Moonheart.

This seemed to surprise the dragon. He looked at them suspiciously for a moment, then said, "An odd group for the Queen to send on a mission."

"We were fewer when we started," said Moonheart. "Others . . . joined us along the way."

"What, precisely, is this mission?" hissed Ebillan. Distrust dripped like venom from his words.

Moonheart nodded toward Cara. "This child seeks the Wanderer, in order to bring her back to Luster."

"What does she have to do with me?" The dragon's tail was writhing faster now, knotting about itself, almost as if it were a separate creature. Suddenly he thrust his head forward. A broad crest sprang up around his neck, snapping out so fast it made Cara jump.

Moonheart stood his ground without flinching. "According to the calculations of the Geomancer, the girl's path lies through your cave," he said quietly.

Ebillan threw back his head and roared in fury, sending another column of fire shooting straight above him. "*Through my cave!* You expect me to let this . . . this *human* enter my home?"

"It is the Queen's wish that the child be given free passage," said Moonheart.

"What the Queen wishes is of little interest to me. She's your queen, not mine." The dragon dropped to a crouch, much like a cat about to spring. His tail writhed more wildly than ever. "This is my territory, and I do *not* welcome trespassers, sent by the Queen or not. Those who set foot here pay with their lives."

The sinuous neck reared back. It was about to shoot forward when Cara stepped up beside Moonheart and cried, "Stop!" The word seemed to come from somewhere deep within her, rising from her belly and scorching her throat.

The dragon blinked at her in astonishment. "You speak our tongue?"

It was only then that Cara realized she had addressed Ebillan in the language of the dragons. Smiling slightly, she said, "I have been given the gift of tongues by the Lady Firethroat, who considers me a friend of dragons. I do not think she would take it kindly were she to find that you had eaten me."

Ebillan settled back on his haunches. His tail still writhed, but a little less rapidly now. "Why didn't you tell me this to begin with?"

"I didn't know you were so lacking in courtesy that I would have to claim my dragon friendship merely to save my life."

"Yike!" muttered the Squijum, tightening his grip on her neck. "Be nice!"

"I have little love for humans," muttered Ebillan, sounding slightly embarrassed.

"I do not seek your love," replied Cara sharply.

225

"Just as well," said Ebillan, and now sarcasm dripped like flame from his words, "as you have little chance of earning it. But what, then, *do* you want?"

"Only what Moonheart has already stated: the right to pass through your cave in order to return to my grandmother's home. I do not seek this boon without offering you something in return."

"Ah," sighed the dragon, sounding almost happy. "You wish to bargain."

"I *offer* to bargain," replied Cara. Reaching into her pack, she closed her fingers over the enormous jewel that Grimwold had given her. She longed to keep it so she could try to see her mother in its crimson depths again. But it had been given to her for this purpose, for bargaining with the dragon. So she pulled it forth and displayed it on her palm, even though doing so felt like taking out a piece of her own heart.

Medafil, standing behind her, sighed when he saw it. "Pretty!" he whispered. *"Pretty!"*

Ebillan's eyes widened in interest. "Very pretty indeed." He extended a claw to take it.

Cara pulled her hand back. "Do we have a bargain?"

The dragon's nostrils flared. "I wish to examine the offer."

Cara hesitated. Lightfoot, who was standing close behind her, whispered, "You can trust him. You have to trust him."

"Indeed she does," said Ebillan. "Don't forget, girl, that I could easily kill you — all of you — and simply take the jewel if I really wanted to. But that is not the dragon way. Now, let me see it."

She stepped toward him, holding up her hand. With talons that looked like burnished metal, he lifted the jewel delicately from her palm.

"Very pretty," said Ebillan again. Then he dropped it back into her hand. "But I think you can do better."

The surge of relief that Cara felt at not having to give up the jewel was quickly replaced by confusion and a touch of anger. "What's wrong with it?" she asked, trying to keep her distress out of her voice. If the dragon wouldn't take this fabulous jewel, what else could she possibly offer him?

"Nothing is wrong with it," said Ebillan smoothly. "In fact, it is flawless. But I believe you can do better."

Cara thought for a moment, then pulled M'Gama's ring from her finger. Hoping the Geomancer would forgive her, she said, "This was a gift from a friend. It is a piece of great beauty, but even more, it is close to my heart. To me, it has much value."

Ebillan took the ring and studied it. "Interesting, but not good enough." Returning the ring to her hand, he added, "Hold on to it, though. It may be of use to you someday."

"How?" asked Cara eagerly as she returned the ring to her finger.

Ebillan snorted. "I am not an oracle. You will have to discover that for yourself. Now, do you have anything else to bargain with, or are you ready to turn around and go?"

For a moment Cara feared that all was lost. Then she remembered the glowing sphere Medafil had given her. She glanced back at the gryphon. Hoping he would not be angry, she reached into her pocket and pulled it forth.

"This is not only beautiful, it is useful," she said. Her words were rueful, for she had planned to use the bauble herself to light her way through darkness for the rest of her life. Twisting the sphere as Medafil had taught her, she expanded it until it was nearly a foot across and looked like a small moon glowing in her hands.

"Very clever," said Ebillan. He took it from her, easily gripping it between two claws, despite its size. To her surprise, the sphere continued to glow, reflecting off the burnished surface of the dragon's talons. He examined it for a moment, then returned it to her hands. "Charming, but I have little need for such a light since I can provide my own."

"Arrogant dragon," muttered Medafil angrily.

Ebillan rolled an eye in the gryphon's direction but did not bother to respond. Instead, he said again to Cara, "Do you have anything else?"

"No," she replied angrily, "I don't!"

Then, her heart sinking, she realized that she did, indeed, have one more item that the dragon might accept. It was a minor thing compared to the others, but closest of all to her heart, even more precious than the sphere, the ring, the jewel.

Slowly, sorrowfully, she reached into her pack and took out Medafil's second gift to her. She heard a little cry of sorrow from Jacques as she brought forth the shell that held her grandmother's voice. Ebillan, however, snorted contemptuously at the sight.

Cara held in a flash of anger. "Though this is more humble," she said enticingly, "it carries a special beauty

229

and is more dear to me than anything else I have offered."

Looking at her with new interest, the dragon took the shell.

"Hold it to your ear," Cara whispered.

Ebillan did as she directed. After a moment he closed his eyes and nodded. The hint of a smile appeared at the corners of his vast, scaly mouth.

Faintly, very faintly, Cara could hear her grandmother's voice singing the now familiar words of "Song of the Wanderer." M'Gama's ring flickered on her finger. It was all Cara could do to keep herself from reaching forward to snatch the shell from Ebillan, to tell him that he couldn't have it after all. She prayed he would reject it, feeling that giving it up was like giving up her closest link to her grandmother.

Then she retracted the prayer, knowing that giving up the shell might be the only way to regain her grandmother.

The dragon put down the shell and sighed. "It will do," he said softly.

Throat tight, heart aching, Cara nodded and whispered, "Then it is yours."

CHAPTER NINETEEN

THE TINKER'S DIVERSION

Ebillan's cave was halfway up a stony mountain. Since the black dragon was much smaller than Firethroat and had no interest in carrying them anyway, they had to walk the entire distance across the bleak and blistering territory, which took them nearly a week.

Finder led the group now, picking a safe way across the treacherous lands of the Northern Waste through some process that only he understood. By the end of the second day, even Belle had expressed a grudging admiration for the skill with which he steered them away from sinkholes and gas vents — a skill that became more obvious when he had started down one path and then abruptly turned back only moments before a gout

231

of vile-smelling flame erupted from the ground, sending rocks the size of Cara's head several dozen feet in the air.

Every evening at sunset Cara made another mark on her counting stick. When they reached the foothills that led to Ebillan's mountain home, only four days remained until the beginning of autumn and the end of the cave's usefulness as her point of passage.

With her goal so close and time so short, Cara found herself nearly frantic with impatience at being forced to trudge along a seemingly endless path. She watched the sky anxiously. The days were growing shorter; even more than her wooden calendar, they assured her that the first day of autumn was nearly upon them. She was terrified of arriving too late, of finding that she would not be able to use the cave as a transit to her grandmother's home after all.

"I can fly you if need be," offered Medafil.

"A noble suggestion, and one we may yet need," said Moonheart. "But we do still have a little time, and I would rather Cara not enter Ebillan's home without all of us to guard her."

"You don't think he'll betray us, do you?" she asked.

"Dragons claim to be bound by their word," said Moonheart. "Even so, I would just as soon not push our luck on that front too hard."

And so they trudged onward.

Though Thomas's cart moved easily over the foothills, when they reached the base of the mountain itself two days later he folded it down to its smallest size — no bigger than a man's wallet — and tucked it into one of his pockets.

"Well," he said, squaring his shoulders, "a tinker's trade takes him many places. Even so, this is one spot in Luster I had never planned to visit. Ah, well. Upward, friends!"

And up they went.

It was the next-to-last day of summer.

Ebillan was lolling at the mouth of his cave when the group arrived. They were exhausted by the climb and ravenously hungry as well, since they had found little to eat during the final stage of their journey.

"I wondered if you would make it," said the dragon casually. "Perhaps you are more serious about this trip than I realized."

"If I weren't serious, you wouldn't have that shell right now," snapped Cara, in no mood for the dragon's rudeness.

"And if I weren't kinder than you think, *you* would be nothing more than a bit of well-grilled meat," replied the dragon smoothly. "I'm tempted to simply return your shell and tell you to go back the way you came. I don't need your snippiness here in my home."

The Dimblethum growled. Cara, repenting her rash words and terrified that she might have ruined the bargain, put a cautioning hand on his thick arm.

The uncomfortable silence that hung between Cara and Ebillan was broken, unexpectedly, by Thomas.

"You don't happen to have anything that needs fixing, do you?" asked the Tinker in a cheerful voice. "Something in the treasure pile that's a little bent and worn, perhaps?"

"What are you talking about?" asked the dragon. Though his voice was surly, it was clear that he was intrigued.

"My trade," said Thomas. "I am a traveling tinker. I mend things. It's my job. Knowing dragons — I have met a few in my day; in fact Fah-Leing is rather a friend of mine — it wouldn't surprise me if you might not have need of my services."

The expression on Ebillan's face was unreadable.

"I can fix practically anything," continued the Tinker encouragingly.

The dragon made a noise deep in his throat. "All right," he said at last. "Come inside."

They entered the cave, which was rank with the smell of sulfur.

"Wait here," said the dragon. Then he turned and headed for the back of the cave.

The sound of Ebillan's scales slithering across the stone floor made Cara shiver. She took Medafil's sphere from her pack and twisted it between her hands until it was about half a foot wide. Its pearly light revealed two openings at the back of the cave. Ebillan vanished into the one on the left.

"Big hotmouth bad ptooie!" muttered the Squijum once the dragon was out of sight.

"Shhhh," cautioned Lightfoot. "His ears may be better than you think."

"And you're the perfect size for a quick snack," added Belle, glaring at the Squijum.

While they were talking, Thomas sidled over to Cara. "If I can get him distracted, and I think I can, head for the back of the cave and go on through to your home. It may be your only chance."

"Won't he be furious?"

"Not if I do my work well enough. And time is precious. We can't waste any more of it. Shhh! He's coming back!"

At first, Cara thought Ebillan hadn't brought anything with him. But when he reached them, he opened his mouth. Out fell a gem-studded goblet made of gold and so big Cara would have had to use both hands to hold it. One side was torn by a jagged split, as if the goblet had been pulled apart by some great force.

Thomas bent to pick it up. "Ow!" he cried. Standing, he began passing it from hand to hand. "Still hot," he explained.

"Fix it," said Ebillan.

"Your wish is my command," replied the Tinker so smoothly that Cara couldn't tell if he was being sarcastic or not.

He placed the cup gently on the floor, then began to

unfold his cart. "Convenient sort of thing, isn't it?" he asked, glancing up at Ebillan as he worked.

The dragon nodded, obviously astonished—something Cara would have thought impossible.

Once the cart was at full size, Thomas went inside. Cara could hear the clatter of tools as he rummaged around. "All set," he said happily, reappearing a few minutes later. "Now, Ebillan, if you could warm this up for me again. Just a bit! I only want to soften the metal."

Heating things "just a bit" turned out not to be something that came easily to the dragon. Finally Thomas discovered that, using a pair of tongs, he could soften the metal of the goblet by holding it inside one of Ebillan's nostrils. Soon the musical *clink* of the Tinker's tools was echoing from the stony walls of Ebillan's cave.

"Beautiful piece," said Thomas as he worked. "What happened to it, anyway?"

"I'd rather not say," growled the dragon.

"Probably did it himself," muttered Lightfoot, who was standing next to Cara.

Ebillan hissed angrily. "You forget yourself, unicorn.

237

My hearing is indeed better than you think. But you are right. I did do it myself. This cup was the cup of my heart. From it I drank the flaming dragonwine that is used in our pledging ceremony. With it I pledged myself to the Lady Nakreema."

"What happened to it?" asked Cara, feeling a tug of sympathy for the dragon in spite of his nastiness.

The flames flickering around Ebillan's nostrils grew brighter. "Long ago, even before the unicorns left Earth, the dragons began to flee to another world. Their reasons were much the same. Earth was becoming hostile to magic, and to magic's children. And they were being hunted, though not so fiercely as the unicorns later were by Beloved and her descendants.

"A magician named Bellenmore—the same one who later helped the unicorns—opened a gate for us. Not all fled. Some of us refused to leave our home, refused to let the humans force us out. Nakreema and I argued about whether to leave. She insisted we had to go. I, being stubborn, insisted on staying. Finally she left without me. I swore a dragon oath that I would see her again, that either I would come for her if things got better, or go to live in that other world myself if things on Earth got worse."

He turned his head away from them. When he spoke again, his voice was soft, like a whisper of flame. "Finally, of course, I did have to leave. But I had waited too long, decided too late, and though dragons can move between worlds, the gate to this new world was closed to us by the very magic that had opened it. Thus when the last seven dragons of Earth—Firethroat, Redrage, Fah-Leing, Master Bloodtongue, Graumag, Bronzeclaw, and myself—finally admitted defeat, and agreed that we had to flee as well, Luster was the only choice left to us."

"A tragic story," murmured Jacques mournfully.

Ebillan swung his head back. "Luster is not my home! That other world, the world where my lost love lives, is not home. *Earth* is home. But Earth, like my love, is lost to me. No dragon can live there now. Too much of the magic has been drained, and we would quickly sicken and die. Even if not, we would be hunted and killed—or, even worse, imprisoned. Do you wonder, human child, that I have little love for your kind?"

He lifted his head and shot forth a gout of flame. It struck the cave's ceiling, then spread across it and down the walls. For one terrifying moment Cara thought it would engulf them all. But Ebillan closed his mouth, and the flame vanished. He dropped his head to the floor. "I tore that cup as a sign of my own broken oath," he whispered sadly. "I did it in a moment of rage and sorrow. Now I repent of my rashness and wish to have it repaired."

Thomas looked up. "I shall do my best," he said. Then, putting his tongue firmly between his teeth, which he did whenever he wanted to concentrate, the Tinker returned his attention to the goblet.

Ebillan settled before him, watching the work with fascination.

Cara stood back, watching as well—watching the dragon watch the Tinker. She was torn about what to do, wanting to take advantage of the opening Thomas had offered, yet terrified that if she did, it would put her friends in jeopardy.

And outside, the sun was sinking toward the horizon, bringing an end to the next to the last day of summer.

Thomas glanced in her direction and seemed startled to see she was still there. He motioned toward the back of the cave with his head, urging her to go.

She placed a hand on Lightfoot's shoulder. "Thomas is doing all this so that I can slip away," she told him, speaking mind to mind. "I'm going to go through now."

"Do you think that is wise?" he asked fretfully.

Almost without her thinking about it, Cara moved her fingers to the gold chain that held the amulet around her neck. She glanced around. Ebillan's eyes were still fixed on Thomas and the golden cup. "It's now or never," she thought to Lightfoot.

"Go in safety," he replied. "Come back soon."

Moving silently, as silently as she had on the night when she and her grandmother were pursued into St. Christopher's by the Hunter she later discovered to be her father, Cara slipped toward the back of the cave.

She peered into the opening Ebillan had entered, the one on the left.

In the distance she could see the glitter of gold.

She stepped to the right.

A short passage led to a smaller cave. It was made of crystal, just as M'Gama had said.

Still moving silently, Cara made her way to the cave. Entering it, she felt as if she had stepped into a diamond. The faceted walls caught the light of Medafil's sphere, reflecting it around her until the brilliance was almost painful. Quickly she twisted the sphere down to marble size and tucked it into her pocket.

Now the crystal cave was dark and silent. Feeling slightly guilty yet at the same time wildly excited, she clutched the amulet, then whispered the spell that would return her to Earth.

"Luster, let me go."

The world swirled green around her. She felt as if she were falling, then as if she were being blown across time by the breath of God. How many minutes, hours, days went by, she could not guess.

Then, so suddenly it left her blinking, she was standing in the kitchen of the house she had shared with her grandmother during the last year.

Luster was gone. She was back on Earth at last.

She glanced around. The kitchen was clean and tidy, just as her grandmother always kept it.

That was a good sign, but not proof. Part of her was still terrified that her grandmother might be gone, that this might be someone else's house now. What would she do then?

She slipped the chain back over her neck and tucked the amulet under her shirt.

She thought about calling out, then decided against it. She didn't want to startle Grandmother Morris with her sudden arrival—or possibly alert some new tenant to the fact that there was an intruder.

But what was the best thing to do now? For all that she had thought of this moment, ached for it, worked toward it, she was not sure how to handle it.

Torn between eagerness and dread, Cara moved to the door that led to the living room. Cautiously, silently, she swung it open.

A woman stood by the window, gazing into the night below. At the sound of Cara's entrance, she turned.

Cara cried out in horror.

CHAPTER TWENTY

BELOVED

"Welcome, wandering child," whispered the woman. She winced and closed her eyes, as if experiencing some horrible pain. After a moment the spasm passed. Opening her eyes again, she said, "I have been waiting for you to return, my many-times great-granddaughter."

Heart pounding, chest tight, throat so dry she could hardly speak, Cara whispered, "Where is my grand-mother?"

"She is wandering, of course. Just as you have been doing. Since she isn't here, I thought I would come and wait for you instead."

A terrible emptiness seemed to swallow Cara. To come all this way and find that her grandmother was gone seemed too much to bear. But then, it would have been even worse to find her a prisoner of Beloved. Fighting to speak calmly, she said, "Is my grandmother safe?"

Beloved shrugged. "I expect so. I don't really care. It's you I'm interested in."

"Me?" asked Cara nervously.

"I've come to take you away with me, dearest. Remember, I am your grandmother, too, though many times farther back. It is time for you to join us, child. Time for you to take your place in our family."

Beloved smiled and took a step toward Cara, then winced again. Even in pain her pale skin was smooth, her features unutterably lovely. Her winter-white hair, curling and wispy like a unicorn's mane, hung well below her waist. The gray irises of her eyes were cold and looked like stone, though in their centers the pupils blazed a hot, terrifying red.

Cara backed away. Without intending to, she began to lift her hand to her neck, reaching toward the amulet. The hungry flicker in Beloved's eyes made her stop. Of course! Beloved wanted the amulet. Her father had told her as much, told her that when Beloved had it, she would be able to open her own gate into Luster, and lead the Hunt into the very world where the unicorns had fled to be safe.

Cara's mind began to race. She had to keep the amulet away from Beloved. But how? She thought, briefly, of trying to fling it through the window. Her heart flinched at the thought; in doing so, she would lock herself out of Luster, too.

She might have done it anyway, only Beloved stood between her and the window, and it seemed likely that if she tried the woman would somehow intercept the amulet.

Her second thought was that she should simply slip back into Luster. But she feared that if she did, Beloved might come with her. She was fairly certain that was how her father had gotten into Luster the last time.

That might not be all bad. Maybe once they had Beloved in Luster they could — what? Kill her? Cara couldn't imagine the unicorns doing that, though Beloved had been responsible for the death of so many unicorns. Imprison her? Cure her? Put her to sleep forever, like the Hunter who had attacked Moonheart all those years ago in the cave in England?

246

Or would she run amok, cause destruction beyond imagining? Cara had no idea how powerful Beloved was, how much magic she controlled. Once in Luster might she be able to summon the Hunters, open a door for them to invade?

"You seem frightened," said Beloved gently. "I'm not going to hurt you, child."

"You'd hurt the unicorns if you could."

Beloved's red eyes blazed, but she kept her voice soft, almost a purr. "There is a great deal that you don't understand," she murmured. Another spasm of pain twisted her face.

"Where is my grandmother?" asked Cara again. "What have you done with her?"

"I told you, she is wandering."

"Where? I want to know *where!*"

Beloved smiled. "Give me the amulet, and I'll tell you."

Cara gasped and felt as if Beloved had somehow managed to reach inside and grab her own heart. Was this what it would come down to? Trade the amulet for her grandmother? The unicorns for the Wanderer?

247

She knew at once what her grandmother would want, and shook her head. "I can't do that."

Beloved shrugged, as if it was of little matter to her.

Cara stared at the woman, trying to understand her. If only Beloved could know the unicorns the way she did, could see how kind and good they were, maybe she would let go of her quest for vengeance.

"The unicorns are my friends," she said softly. "They're not bad, like you think. They're not —"

"Quiet!" shrieked Beloved. "You miserable brat, who do you think you are to tell me about the unicorns? What do you know, what can you know, in the tiny amount of time you've been alive? Did the unicorns kill *your* father? Did they curse *you* with a pain-laced life that goes on and on, never letting you die?" Her features writhed, and then she gained control of them once more. "The unicorns are nice," she simpered. "The unicorns are kind. You driveling nitwit. What can you possibly know about their evil, their deceit, their vileness?"

Panting, Beloved lunged toward her.

Cara ducked aside. Beloved spun and, with astonishing speed, lunged again. This time she caught Cara by the arm. They tumbled to the floor together.

"I *will* have that amulet!" shrieked Beloved, clawing at Cara's neck.

Cara grabbed the woman's wrists and tried to push them back, but Beloved was strong, terribly strong. Then another spasm of pain struck. Beloved shuddered and cried out, and her grip weakened. Cara wrenched herself away, then rolled over so that her face was to the floor. Tucking her fists against her jaw, her arms tight against her sides, she pressed down, trying to meld herself with the carpet.

Beloved pulled at her arms, and then her hair. "Roll over!" she cried. *"Roll over!"*

Cara pushed herself down even harder, praying for the moment to end, for Beloved to vanish. But like a madwoman, she continued to claw at Cara. Then, suddenly, the attack stopped. For an instant Cara thought Beloved had given up. Then she felt her hands on her ankles. Before Cara could do a thing about it, Beloved had flipped her over.

Cara pulled back her feet, then thrust them forward as hard as she could, catching Beloved in the chest. Eyes widening in astonishment, the white-haired woman staggered back against the wall. Cara scrambled to her feet and headed for the window. She *would* fling the amulet out, even if it meant she could never get back to Luster herself. But she hesitated for just a moment, stopped by a new fear: What if someone else found it, someone who shouldn't go to Luster?

They wouldn't know how to use it, she told herself.

The instant's hesitation was all Beloved needed. She hurled herself across the room and grabbed Cara from behind. With her tight embrace pinning Cara's arms to her sides, Beloved began to whisper in the girl's ear. "You mustn't be like this," she crooned. "Grandmother Beloved doesn't like it. Be good, and Grandmother Beloved will be good to you. Be nice, and Grandmother Beloved will be nice to you. I'll teach you secrets you never imagined, Cara. There is so much waiting for you, child. Things you've never dreamed of, things the unicorns would never have told you about." She paused as another wave of pain shuddered through her, and then went on again, her voice low and seductive. "I know deep and secret places in the world, unsuspected beauties, mysteries beyond anything most humans can even guess at. Give yourself to me, Cara. Let your blood answer its call. You are one of my children. You *are* a Hunter, and it's not right, not good, for you to resist me like this. Just relax, dearheart. Relax and let Grandmother Beloved take care of everything for you. No need to think, no need to worry. Relax. Relax."

Her voice was soothing, hypnotic. Against her will, Cara began to sag in the woman's arms. She could feel one of Beloved's hands creeping toward the chain that held the amulet — could feel it, but didn't seem to be able to do anything about it.

"Relax," whispered the voice, which came to her as through a fog. "Relax into the mystery and the beauty that only I can give you. Relax, and when you do, I can take you back to your mother. Relax and —"

"That's enough!" A familiar voice, strong and sharp, cut through the velvet of Beloved's words. The woman's grip faltered, and Cara slithered out of her arms.

"Jacques!" cried Cara. "How did you —" She broke off. Not only was her grandfather standing in the doorway that led to the kitchen, but next to him was Lightfoot.

A new wave of terror washed over her. "Lightfoot, what are you doing here? Go. *Go!*"

Her words were drowned in Beloved's shriek of rage. "To me, my children!"

From the hallway, where they had been waiting in silence, rushed seven men. They were dressed in black and armed with glistening swords.

Cara cried out in fear and confusion when she saw that the man at the front of the group was her father.

Lightfoot reared back and trumpeted a challenge, the tip of his horn grazing the ceiling.

The men raced toward him. His hooves flashed forward, raining silver blows among them. The attackers dropped back, but not before one managed to slash open Lightfoot's side with his sword. Crimson and silver blood spurted from the wound.

Jacques hurtled forward in a series of handsprings, which ended with his feet smashing into the chin of one of the Hunters. The man let out a startled cry, then crumpled to the floor.

"One down!" crowed Jacques, looking happier than Cara had ever seen him.

Two others turned toward him. He began to leap and spin like some demented dervish, his agility astonishing for someone his age. One of the men rushed forward. Jacques ducked underneath his arm, came up behind him as he rushed past, and gave him a solid kick in the back of the head that sent him sprawling.

"Fools rush in," Jacques murmured in satisfaction.

Now half the men had turned their attention toward the old tumbler. The others, swords raised and ready, stood facing Lightfoot.

Though Cara had started forward when she saw Lightfoot wounded, Beloved had again grabbed her from behind. Now, despite her desperate struggles, the woman held her fast.

Bugling in fury, Lightfoot lunged toward them, plowing past the men, knocking two of them down, ignoring the second and third wounds that scored his sides. Cara struggled to break free.

The room was a madhouse of sound and fury, the battle made awkward by the close quarters. The men bumped into furniture, scrambled over it, leaped over it, stumbled and fell over it. One screamed in pain, then fell writhing to the floor when Lightfoot's flashing hooves struck his arm and snapped the bone.

"Enough!" cried Beloved in a voice so powerful it

sliced through the chaos and turmoil, so commanding that all eyes turned toward her.

All eyes save Cara's.

For Beloved held her from behind. The woman had one arm around Cara's neck. Her other hand, which clutched a silver dagger, was poised above Cara's heart.

CHAPTER TWENTY-ONE

BETRAYAL

The battle stopped. Jacques and Lightfoot stood without moving. Three of the men lay moaning on the floor. One of the men still standing raised his sword as if to plunge it into Lightfoot's side.

"Not now, Marcus," snapped Beloved. "Better to do it later, with ceremony and ritual. You'll waste too much magic this way. Kenneth, bring the binding."

A tall man with reddish-gold hair stepped toward Lightfoot. From his hand dangled a golden bridle.

When the unicorn shied away, Beloved said sharply, "Careful, beast!"

The woman's voice was ragged with pain, and Cara could feel the shudder that rippled through her. She tried to take advantage of the moment to squirm free of Beloved's grasp. It did no good. Beloved tightened her grip and brought the tip of her silver dagger to rest directly against Cara's chest.

Lightfoot, watching, shook his head. "Be still, Cara," he whispered.

She slumped back and watched helplessly as the golden bridle was placed over his head. To her horror, the moment it was on him she could see him relax, falling calm and docile under the bridle's spell. She felt as if all hope had been ripped from her heart.

"Good," murmured Beloved. "Now he is ours, to do with as we will." Then, as if she had barely noticed Jacques until now, she said, "Ian, bind the old man. Tightly!"

Ian. Ian Hunter. Cara's father.

Her father, who hadn't even acknowledged her presence.

That's all right, she thought fiercely. *He's not my father anymore. I don't want him!*

Even so, it hurt that it was her father who pushed Jacques into a chair, her father who pulled the old man's hands behind his back and bound them with black cord, her father who bound his feet as well, tying them to the legs of the chair so that he couldn't even hobble away.

Bitterness rose within her, so strong she could taste it. How could he do these things?

"Good," said Beloved. She lowered the knife and stepped away from Cara. "Now, Great-granddaughter, let us try talking again. There are things you need to know, things you do not understand. Sit down. I want to take a look at our captive."

Cara did as the woman directed — partly because one of the Hunters came to stand beside her to make sure she didn't try to escape.

Beloved walked around Lightfoot, studying him carefully. He stood, docile and unflinching, even when she poked at his wounds. His flanks were drenched in his own blood, silver and scarlet, and the sight was like acid in Cara's eyes. She longed to heal him but could not; longed to save him but didn't know how.

When Beloved was done, her face glowed with triumph. "This is better than I could have hoped for! Do you know what we have here, my children? A unicorn of the royal family. Not merely of royal blood, but next in line for the throne. We have captured Prince Lightfoot himself."

Cara blinked in astonishment. She had known

Lightfoot was the Queen's grandson. But next in line for the throne? How could this be?

Following hard on that question came another, one she had lost track of in the chaos of the fight: *How had Jacques and Lightfoot crossed to Earth?*

She realized it was possible she might never find out because she might never speak to either of them again . . . might never again see them alive.

She blinked back tears, telling herself to keep strong.

Beloved returned to Cara. Reaching down, she hooked a slender finger under the chain that held the amulet. Tugging at it, she pulled the amulet from under Cara's shirt. It rested in her palm, golden and sparkling, the luminous white hair from a unicorn's mane curled beneath its crystal lid.

"Soon," she murmured. "Soon."

Then she dropped the chain.

"Aren't you going to take it?" asked Cara in surprise.

"I will if I have to. But it will do less damage to the magic if you give it to me freely."

Cara snorted.

"Don't be rude, child. I *could* simply take it if I wanted to. Or I could bargain with you — the amulet for the life of one of your friends over there."

Cara felt her head swim. Would she trade the amulet for Jacques or Lightfoot? Of course! Except . . . except if she did, how many more unicorns would die as a result?

"That would be better. But it would be better still," continued Beloved, "if you simply *gave* it to me because you finally understood that what I am doing is right, and that you have been tricked and used by the unicorns."

Her face writhed, and she gasped for breath. The moment passed, and she composed her features again.

"You have been deceived, Cara — fooled into thinking these creatures are kind and compassionate. This is not true. They are brutal and vicious."

Jacques leaned forward. "That's a lie, a total — "

His words were cut off by a backhanded blow from Marcus.

Beloved sighed. "It is hard to reason with you with all this distraction, Great-grandchild." She glanced up at the man standing beside Cara's chair. "Anders, you and Marcus take the old man into the next room. I don't want to hear from him again."

"Jacques!" cried Cara as the two men picked up the chair to which her grandfather was bound and carried him into the kitchen.

The door slammed shut.

"Why are you doing these things?" asked Cara. "Why won't you leave us in peace?"

Beloved looked down at Cara. In the woman's stony eyes there was, at last, some look of humanity — traces of pity, of anger, of sorrow.

"Listen to me carefully, child. I am older than you can imagine, so do not think you can speak to me of things you scarcely understand. I have lived an eternity etched by pain, staggered through centuries with a fire gnawing at my heart. After the unicorns fled from Earth, I was lost. Where could I turn my anger, how seek my revenge? I tried for a time equal to the lives of many mortals to find a way into Luster so I could lead my children there to finish what we had begun, but I was blocked at every turn. Finally weariness overcame me, and I let my efforts lapse. I couldn't die, but I had nothing to live for. I wept and I brooded, haunted by the image of the unicorn that had pierced my heart, then killed my father. And my heart throbbed in constant agony from the piece of horn that lances and heals it with every breath I take."

She fell silent for a moment, staring out the window. Almost against her will, Cara said, "And then?"

Beloved smiled, a cold and terrifying sight. "And then you happened."

Cara fought to keep her voice from trembling. "What do you mean?"

"I was only vaguely aware of your father; he was but one of thousands of my descendants scattered around the world. I kept an eye on all of them, of course, but in my weariness I had ceased to choose new ones to train in the Hunt. What was the point? My enemies had fled, and I could not get at them. All gone." She paused and smiled. "Well, all save one. There is almost always one unicorn here on Earth. The Guardian of Memory, they call him. Sometimes" — here she paused again and closed her eyes in ecstasy — "ah, sometimes my Hunters would find that one and slay him! Then, for a moment, my heart would be at peace. But another would come. Always, sooner or later, another would come. What I wanted, *craved,* was a path into Luster itself. Only then could the Hunt be properly concluded. Only then could I finish my job and rest. Only then would the wound in my heart finally heal for good and all.

"We sought the gates, but could not find them. However, there was one other possibility. I knew there was a key, an amulet here on Earth with which I could open a new gate to Luster. I knew, too, that it belonged to Ivy Morris. But we could not locate it. She would not stay put, and her wandering defeated my efforts to find her. Until Ian, dear Ian, married your mother. I did not realize, at first, that one of my children had connected to the family of the Wanderer. It was only when you were sick, and your grandmother summoned a unicorn to heal you, that I understood what luck had come my way.

"But the very night that I made contact with your father, that I came to tell him his true heritage, your grandmother disappeared, taking you with her. Oh, the Wanderer was a clever one. She knew I was after her. After you. After the amulet."

Cara groaned. So it was true. Her grandmother *had* stolen her from her parents.

Or had she? Could she trust what Beloved was telling her? Was it possible she was lying, even now?

"Your father was wild in his grief over losing you. But it also proved to him that what I had told him about the unicorns and their evil was true."

"But the unicorn cured me!" protested Cara.

"Because the Wanderer summoned him," repeated Beloved, speaking very slowly, as if she felt Cara had failed to understand something utterly simple. "The unicorns have their human allies, friends who have traded their duty and obligation for a bit of glamour and magic. Of course he cured you! They wanted to use you — use you to get at *me.*"

Cara blinked. That couldn't be true, could it? Yet she knew how the unicorns hated and feared Beloved.

She shook her head, trying to drive away the poison Beloved was pouring into her ears. If the unicorns wanted to use her to get at Beloved, they would have been able to do it long before this.

"Where is my mother?" she asked. "What have you done with her?"

"Your mother is somewhere safe," said Beloved. Then, coaxingly, she added, "I can take you to her, you know."

Cara felt her heart leap. She glanced at her father. His face remained still, unreadable.

"Oh, it's going to be so lovely," continued Beloved. "You can be with your parents again, just like you've always wanted, Cara. You'll be home at last, and your heart will be able to rest." She clutched her own heart, her ever-wounded, ever-healing heart. "As will mine. For just as you will gain your heart's desire, so will I when I fling wide the gate and send my children to Luster. For am I not the Ravager? Is it not written in my stars — the very stars through which I have twice made contact with you — that I shall be the one to bring the murdering beasts to justice?"

Cara gasped. "The Ravager! The constellation! That was how you were able to get to me!"

Beloved went on as if she had not heard. "Oh, how the blood will flow when the Ravager finally enters Luster! And once the Hunt is done, once the unicorns are *all* gone, the fire in my heart will be gone, too. Then, finally, I will be free!"

Her eyes were wild now, glazed with the passion of the Hunt as she imagined it. "All I need is the amulet. Give it to me, Cara. Give it to me and you can join me, join your father and find your mother. We'll be together, all of us."

Lightfoot stood, impassive, held by the magic of the golden bridle.

Cara turned away.

"Look at me!" screeched Beloved. She reached out, grabbed Cara by the chin, forced her to stare directly into those blazing eyes. "It is time, child; time to give me the amulet. Give it, or I will take it. Give it freely and join us, or have it ripped away and be cast away yourself, away from the Hunters, away from your family, away from your own blood. Choose, Cara. Choose now. For I *will* have that amulet, what ever way you decide. I'll have it, with you or without you. The unicorns are going to die anyway. Are you going to join me, or not? Do you want — "

"Stop!" cried Cara, clamping her hands over her ears. "Stop!"

"No!" shrieked Beloved. "The time for stopping is past. Choose! Choose now! My blood runs in your veins, Cara. You are part of an ancient story. It is time for you to take your place and play your role. I was a child when it began. You are the child born to help me end it."

Cara wrenched herself away. Beloved lunged at her, clutched the amulet.

"Let me go!" cried Cara. "I choose the unicorns. *I choose the unicorns!*"

Beloved hissed in fury, wound her fist in the amulet's

chain, pulled at it, choking Cara as she tried to wrench it from her neck.

"That's enough," said a deep voice.

A pair of hands grabbed Beloved from behind.

Cara looked up in astonishment. Then she closed her eyes and whispered, "Thank you . . . Daddy."

Her father stood there, holding Beloved by the arms. Kenneth, the only other Hunter who had remained standing in the room, was crumpled on the floor. Lightfoot, no longer restrained by the golden bridle, stood guarding the door to the room where the other two men had taken Jacques.

Beloved, wild with fury, struggled in Ian Hunter's arms. "Traitor!" she shrieked as he pried her fingers from the amulet's chain. "Betrayer!"

"Perhaps," he said grimly. "But was I not betrayed myself when I lost my daughter to the struggle between you and the Wanderer? I lost her again in Firethroat's cave because of your teachings and my own stubborn blindness. I would have lost her a third time tonight. But her courage has opened my eyes."

The muscles in his lean arms rippled as he forced Beloved around so that she was facing him, moving his hands so that they gripped her wrists. Her fingers arched like claws, straining for his eyes. But he held her tight, and she could not reach him.

"It is enough, Grandmother Beloved," he said between clenched teeth. "Let it go. Let it go!"

She spat in his face. He drew back, startled. In his moment of surprise, Beloved broke free of his grip and raked her fingers down his cheek, leaving four streaks of blood.

"I'll let nothing go, you spineless pup!" she shrieked. Then, suddenly, she collapsed, falling limp into his arms. "All these years," she moaned. "All these years! Oh, Ian, Ian, how could you betray me like this?"

Tenderly, Ian Hunter lowered the ancient woman to the floor, where she curled in a miserable heap, weeping. Stepping past her, he reached toward his daughter. Cara stretched her hands toward him, tears streaming down her own face as she did.

Before they could embrace, Beloved was on her feet again. "Betrayer!" she cried.

Then she plunged the silver dagger into his back.

CHAPTER TWENTY-TWO

UPSTAIRS

Cara stood frozen with horror, her hands still outstretched to where her father had been standing. Then something deep within, a rage and a strength she had not known she possessed, took over. She launched herself at Beloved. Knocking the knife from the woman's hand, she carried Beloved backward with her momentum. Together, they tumbled to the floor.

Again, Beloved clutched at the amulet. But before she could take it from Cara, Lightfoot entered the fray. Snatching the woman's robe in his teeth, he hauled her from Cara.

With a cry of rage, Beloved ripped away. She threw herself across the floor, toward the silver dagger. Cara was there first. Kicking the blade, she sent it skittering toward the hallway.

The door to the kitchen burst open. Anders and Marcus, the Hunters who had hauled Jacques away, came running in.

Lightfoot turned to face them. Anders, sword in hand, slashed at Lightfoot, but the unicorn was too fast for him and danced nimbly away despite his wounds.

Marcus raced to Beloved, knelt beside her, and whispered urgently to her.

She was on her feet in an instant. "To me!" she cried in triumph. "Come to me, my children!"

Even as she spoke, she hurried to one of the fallen Hunters and stood astride his body.

At her call, Anders backed away from Lightfoot. The unicorn, who had been rearing defiantly, dropped to all fours. He watched the men cautiously. Marcus and Anders each grabbed one of the other men who had been rendered helpless during the first fight — one unconscious, the other unable to walk — and dragged them to Beloved's side.

Cara, with no one to stop her, had also raced to a fallen Hunter. Her father. She knelt beside him, tears streaming down her face. His hand closed over hers, weak but warm, and she felt a surge of relief. He was still alive!

But what was Beloved up to?

When the Hunters were gathered close around her — the last of them had dragged himself to her side — she lifted her hands.

"This round is yours, grandchild," she said, her eyes narrow and filled with hate. "But the battle is not over. In fact, it's just beginning, as you will soon see, my stubborn one."

She spread her arms, encircling the Hunters with her black cloak, which seemed to billow and expand as she lifted her arms. As the cloak swirled around her, she uttered some words in a deep, guttural voice.

With a flash, the group vanished.

"I don't like this," said Lightfoot. "What is she up to?"

"Never mind that now!" cried Cara urgently. "My father is hurt. You are, too, I know. But I think he's dying. Can you heal him?"

Lightfoot hurried to her side.

"The cut is deep and bitter," he said after probing the wound with his horn. "Not only blade but poison is at work here. Even so, I think it can be healed. Though why I should heal a Hunter . . ."

"He saved us!"

"Oh, I know," said Lightfoot wearily. "Another rene-gade. I'll probably end up liking him. Well, let me do my work. You had best go check on your grandfather."

With a throb of guilt, Cara realized she had almost forgotten Jacques. Had the Hunters hurt him? *Killed him?* Longing to stay to make sure her father was prop-erly healed, yet trusting Lightfoot and knowing there was nothing more she could do here, she hurried to the next room.

A cold dread seized her. Jacques, still tied to the chair, sagged in his bonds. His head was slumped onto his chest. Hurrying to his side, she was relieved to find he was still breathing. She saw no blood, no stab wounds. But when she knelt beside him to try to wake him, she noticed an egg-sized lump on the side of his head.

"Poor Grampa," she whispered softly. She set to work untying his bonds. When she had him free, she lowered him gently to the floor. She looked around for something to cushion his head but saw nothing that would work. "I'll be back," she whispered. Then she re-turned to the living room.

Lightfoot was lying on his side, his eyes closed. He lifted his head when he heard her enter. "It's done," he told her quietly. "Your father will live." Then he dropped his head back to the floor, closed his eyes, and slept.

Ian Hunter still lay facedown on the floor. Cara knelt beside him. His color was good, his breathing regular.

She turned her attention to Lightfoot. The slash that had opened his side was longer than her arm but not deep, and the bleeding had stopped. She thought briefly about trying to sew it shut, then decided it would be better to wait for one of the other unicorns to heal it. She returned to the kitchen and got a pan and a towel. She filled the pan with water and soaked the towel. Then she returned to the living room and washed the blood from Lightfoot's side.

That done, she stood and looked around, feeling oddly lonely at being the only one in the house still awake. Lonely and restless. She felt as if there was still more to do. But what? Her grandmother was gone; where, she didn't know. They couldn't return to Luster until the others had recovered. With a sudden surge of dread she wondered if, when they did return, it would be to Ebillan's cave, or somewhere else altogether. Did time pass the same way here on Earth that it did in Luster? Had the world shifted yet? If so, where would the amulet take them?

She felt a restless need to move *now*. To do something. Anything. Finally she remembered that she had been going to get something to cushion Jacques' head. She could do that for her father, too. Eager to do anything that felt useful, she headed for the stairway. The shabby blue carpet that covered the steps seemed immediately familiar despite the time that had passed since she last saw it.

At the top of the stairs, she turned left. When she entered her old bedroom, the sight of it, so comfortable and cozy, so far from the life she had been living, made her stagger. She leaned against the wall, staring at it in wonder. How far away the girl who had once lived here — the girl she had once been — now seemed.

She went to her bed and ran her hand over the bedspread, smiling at its flowers. She had wanted unicorns, cute and cartoony, and had been angry when her grandmother had forbidden the idea. Now that she had seen real unicorns, she understood.

She picked up the single pillow, then frowned. She needed another one, for Jacques. After a moment's hesitation, she headed for her grandmother's room.

Slipping through the door, she turned on the light, then cried out in astonishment.

On the bed lay her grandmother.

Ivy Morris.

The Wanderer.

Calling her grandmother's name, Cara hurried to her side.

The old woman lay perfectly still. She was fully clothed, her hands crossed on her chest, her eyes closed.

She can't be dead! thought Cara. *She* can't *be!*

Tenderly, fearfully, Cara reached out to touch the body.

It was warm!

She remembered Beloved telling her that her grandmother was wandering, and not here. Had she lied? Or had she, in her own strange way, been telling the truth?

Her grandmother was here, but not here.

Was her spirit indeed wandering somewhere else?

If so, where? And how could she be called home? Cara felt herself overwhelmed by a sense of mystery.

"What has she done to you, Gramma?" she whispered, kneeling beside the Wanderer's bed. "What kind of spell has she put you under?"

The Wanderer did not answer.

"Wake up!" cried Cara, shaking her grandmother's shoulders. "WAKE UP! I NEED YOU!"

Ivy Morris lay still and unmoving.

Despair washed over Cara like a wave of blackness. Dropping her head to the bed, she sobbed with a hurt she had not known she could feel anymore.

She remained kneeling beside the bed long after her tears had stopped, whispering to her grandmother, cajoling her, begging her to wake.

The Wanderer made no response.

At last, overwhelmed by loneliness, Cara decided to check on the others again. Clutching the pillow she had taken from her own room, she went downstairs, where she tucked it under her father's head. Then she took a throw pillow from one of the chairs — smaller and less comfortable than those from the beds, but still better than the floor — and carried it to the kitchen, where she tucked it under Jacques' head.

The older man stirred as she moved him. "Cara?" he asked in a hoarse whisper.

"Yes, it's me."

"I'm sorry," he murmured with a tone of gloom deeper than any she had ever heard from him, so deep it was almost painful to listen to. "So sorry."

"For what? You saved me. If you and Lightfoot hadn't arrived when you did, Beloved would have taken me away with her." Then she remembered something she had wondered about earlier. "How did you do that, anyway? Come through to Earth?"

But he had drifted into unconsciousness again and could not answer her.

She stroked his brow for a moment, then left the kitchen and climbed the stairs once again, so weary that she had to drag herself up them. They had come all this way to find her grandmother, and, though found, she was still as lost to them as ever.

Returning to her own room, so familiar yet now so strange, Cara took the chair from her desk and carried it to her grandmother's room. She placed it beside the bed and sat down to keep watch.

She remembered how her grandmother used to do

276

the same for her when she was ill — how she would sit beside the bed and sing to her. Reaching out, Cara put her hand on her grandmother's forehead and began to sing herself. She did the old songs first, the comforting lullabies that had meant so much to her when she was little: "Toora Loora Lura" and "All the Pretty Little Horses" and "Angels Watching Over Me."

She ran through all the ones she could remember, sang them twice, and then a third time, pleased at how many of the words she still knew, oddly sorrowful at how many she had forgotten.

Then, almost without thinking about it, she began another song.

The "Song of the Wanderer."

Her voice high and clear, she sang:

> *Across the gently rolling hills*
> *Beyond high mountain peaks,*
> *Along the shores of distant seas*
> *There's something my heart seeks.*
>
> *But there's no peace in wandering,*
> *The road's not made for rest.*

And footsore fools will never know
What home might suit them best.

The song seemed to speak to her of her own life now, and her voice began to waver on the second verse as longing and sorrow choked her. Tears swam in her eyes, blurring her vision. So she didn't see her grandmother's lips begin to move.

She did, however, feel M'Gama's ring begin to burn on her finger.

Looking down, she saw that it was glowing again, more intensely than ever before. The green grew brighter, brighter still, until it almost hurt her eyes.

Then it pulled her in.

CHAPTER TWENTY-THREE

THE RAINBOW PRISON

Cara felt as if she were falling — felt, indeed, much as she had the moment after she had leaped from the tower of St. Christopher's. Around her was nothing but green, green that swirled and shifted: the light green of spring grass; the deep green of pine needles; the greens of seawater, of apples in early summer, of sunbeams filtering through the forest.

Beyond the green, or from somewhere within it, she could hear a voice, long loved, long lost, dearly familiar — the voice of her grandmother.

> *My heart longs to rest,*
> *My feet yearn to roam.*
> *Shall I wander the world*
> *Or stay safe at home?*

Then, as had happened in M'Gama's underground workroom, Cara heard the plaintive, heartbreaking cry: "Cara, is that you? Oh, come and get me, my child. Come and get me. I am wandering, wandering and so far from home."

"Where are you, Gramma? *Where are you?*"

"Here." The voice drifted to her from out of the swirling green. "Here, in the rainbow prison."

Cara had gone underground with M'Gama, and even deeper underground when they'd traveled with Grimwold. Now she felt as if she were descending yet again, into someplace stranger than she had yet experienced.

The green still swirled around her, misty and insubstantial. Then she noticed a strand of it that looked more solid. Thick as a rope, it twisted and coiled away from her, into the green distance. Looking to see where it went in the other direction, Cara was startled to discover that it ended at her own hand, at M'Gama's ring. She wondered, for an instant, whether it was flowing out of the ring, or coming from somewhere else and flowing into it.

Suddenly she realized the strand was beginning to

fray, green drifting into green. When she grabbed for it with her free hand, her fingers closed over it as if it were made of fog.

"Cara!" called her grandmother's pleading voice. "*Cara!*"

She sounded more distant than ever.

The ring was growing dim. Remembering the other times it had glowed unexpectedly, Cara began to sing.

Instantly the ring glowed more brightly, and the strand of green grew thicker again.

"Sing, Gramma!" Cara called excitedly after she had finished the first verse. "Sing it with me!"

Trying to send her own voice into the swirling green emptiness, pulling the words not from her mind but her heart, she continued:

> *But there's no peace in wandering,*
> *The road's not made for rest.*
> *And footsore fools will never know*
> *What home might suit them best.*

Her heart lifted when she heard her grandmother's voice join her on the chorus:

My heart seeks the hearth,
My feet seek the road.
A soul so divided
Is a terrible load.

My heart longs to rest,
My feet yearn to roam.
Shall I wander the world
Or stay safe at home?

On they sang, and on, until they reached the final verse:

Oh where's the thread that binds me,
The voice that calls me back?
Where's the love that finds me —
And what's the root I lack?

Now the green rope was strong and sturdy, and Cara pulled her way along it. As she did, her grandmother began the song again. Suddenly Cara realized she was no longer pulling herself along the rope. Instead, the rope was pulling her. Faster and faster she moved until the green around her blurred into a solid-seeming wall. And then she was there, beside her grandmother — her true grandmother, not merely the body she lived in.

"I found you!" she cried, surprised to discover that she was weeping. "I've found you at last." She flung herself toward her grandmother, which was the first time she realized that she, too, had left her body behind. She felt a flicker of fear, but it was lost in her joy at finding her grandmother. And though neither of them was wrapped in flesh, the embrace they shared was real and solid.

"Cara," whispered the old woman after a time. "My Cara. I knew you would come for me."

"But where are we?" asked Cara, not raising her head to look.

"I don't know."

It was not merely the words that Cara found terrifying, it was the tone of hopelessness in her grandmother's voice. "How did you get here?" Cara asked, pulling away a little now.

Ivy Morris looked uneasy. "An old enemy sent me," she said at last.

"Was it Beloved?"

Cara's grandmother looked surprised, and somewhat frightened. "I think you have a lot to tell me, grand-daughter."

"That's true for you, too," replied Cara sharply. Then, though she had vowed not to, had promised herself she would hold her questions until this was all over, the words forced themselves out in an angry burst. "Did you really steal me from my parents?"

Ivy Morris flinched back, looking almost terrified. Then her face relaxed. "I should have realized that some of our past would come to light when I sent you to Luster. Yes, dearheart, I did just that."

"But *why?*"

"I suspect you already know the answer."

"All right, I do. What I don't know is why you didn't *tell* me about it. Why did you lie to me all those years, let me think they had abandoned me?"

Her grandmother sighed. "I couldn't bring myself to tell you they were dead — though it might have been kinder if I had."

"But they *weren't* dead!" exploded Cara. "That would still have been a lie. *Why didn't you just tell me the truth?*"

Ivy Morris looked directly at her granddaughter.

Her own eyes deep with sorrow, she whispered, "Because the truth was too heavy a burden to place on you."

Cara started to protest, but her grandmother raised her hands to stop her. "I don't mean it would have been too painful for you to hear — though I think it would have been more painful than you might believe, especially when you were little. No, I mean that *holding* the truth is too painful."

Cara drew back from her grandmother, and in so doing noticed, for the first time, the world around them, which she had ignored in the rush and excitement of their reunion.

It had more solid detail than she had expected.

They stood at the edge of a forest, but a forest greener than any she had ever seen, a forest where not only the leaves but the trunks and branches of the trees were green — as were the rocks, the water, the ground below, the sky above. It reminded her of when she had seen her mother in Grimwold's gem, and everything had been crimson and scarlet.

Ivy Morris gestured to the bank of a stream. "Sit with me," she said. Spectral though it was, her human form was startlingly clear against the green world that stretched around them.

Cara settled beside her. She thrust one foot into the water but felt nothing. Nor, for that matter, could she feel the ground beneath her. Only her grandmother seemed real.

"Secrets are a heavy burden," said Ivy Morris quietly. "More of a burden than I wanted to place on a child. They want to be let out, struggle to be free, beat against the walls of your heart until you ache with the effort of holding them in. But some secrets *are* better left untold."

She turned her head away. When she spoke again, her voice was soft and filled with pain. "Luster is a big secret to carry — so big that more than once I *did* try to share it. But it also turned out to be too big to tell, too big for anyone to believe."

She turned back, looked directly into her granddaughter's eyes. "I have not been close to many people in my life, Cara. Something in me — the same thing that made me a Wanderer, I suppose — makes that hard for me. But a few, a very few, I loved and tried to tell. Their disbelief was painful. Their fear for me, their sense that I had lost my mind, stung my heart. I was even put in a hospital for it once, and had to pretend not to believe the truest thing in my life until I could finally convince the doctors that they had 'cured' me." She laughed ruefully. "I would have just fled to Luster and left them wondering how I had escaped, except that I had been taken without the amulet." She paused, then said thoughtfully, "Or maybe I wouldn't have. It wasn't time for me to return yet. Anyway, given what I knew about trying to tell this secret, what would I have told you, my darling — and how would you have dealt with it?"

Cara sat silent, uncertain how to answer. She remembered the playground teasing she had taken over things that, next to the reality of Luster, were like grains of sand compared to a boulder. "Why didn't you just take me to Luster with you?" she asked at last.

Her grandmother sighed. "And what would you have told your friends when we came back?"

"I mean, why didn't you take me there to live? I would have liked that."

Ivy Morris shook her head sadly. "I couldn't do that until I was ready to return myself. You don't know how

I longed to tell you, Cara. I thought about it almost every day, trying to find the right way, the right time. Then that man began following us — "

"You don't have to pretend. I know it was my father who chased us into St. Christopher's."

Ivy Morris looked startled, then nodded in acceptance. "Then came the night when your father began following us. Suddenly there was no time left to tell you, and I had to send you off unprepared. For that, you have my deepest apologies, my darling.

"After you jumped into Luster, I was left alone in the tower — alone, and lonely. That was a feeling I had not experienced for a long time." She smiled, but it was a tight, painful smile. "Wanderers cannot afford to be lonely. Of course, I was not merely lonely. I was frantic with concern for you — and for the unicorns. What did it mean that your father had discovered us? What did it mean that he had followed you into Luster?

"I should not have gone home after that. I should have moved on at once. I knew that. But there were things I did not want to leave. Foolish, foolish of me. Things tie you down, Cara, and I could not afford to be tied." She sighed. "It wasn't just things. I wanted to be there in case you returned. So I went home." She drew a deep breath. "Beloved was there, waiting for me."

"Did she hurt you?"

"A little. But when it became clear that I did not have the amulet and could not get it, she set my soul wandering free of my body — cast me into this green strangeness with little hope of ever finding my way back. I have roamed the greenness of this place, Cara, pressing at its edges, seeking a way out."

"I heard you calling once, I think," said Cara. "I was in the cave of the Geomancer — "

"M'Gama," whispered Ivy Morris, a strange note in her voice. "Yes, I'm not surprised if my voice reached you in that place. The magic is deep there, and surprising things can happen. Did she help you find your way back to Earth?"

"Yes."

The old woman chuckled dryly. "I'm sure she had mixed feeling about *that!*"

Cara held up her hand to display the band of green on her finger. "It was her ring that brought me to you. It's keyed to the song, I think. It pulled me in, somehow, when you responded to my singing. Oh, I can't believe I found you, Gramma! I've been trying so hard to get back to Earth so I can bring you home to Luster. The Queen wants to see you, to say — "

Cara stopped, the words catching in her throat. What the Queen wanted to say was good-bye. How would her grandmother react to that news? Suddenly Cara began to understand how her grandmother had put off telling her painful truths for so long.

Her thoughts were interrupted by Ivy Morris's whisper. "The Queen," she said softly.

The strands of emotion in her voice — the love and regret, the joy and sorrow, and most of all the longing — were too thick, and far too tangled, for Cara to sort out. "I took her your message, Gramma. I told her, 'The Wanderer is weary.'"

"Truer words were never spoken," said Ivy Morris ruefully.

"She asked me to bring you back so . . ." Cara faltered a second time on the painful thought, then forced herself to go on. "She says she has to see you before she can rest."

Ivy Morris looked stricken. Her voice little more

than a whisper, she asked, "Is she so close to fading, then?"

Cara nodded. "I think she might have been gone already if she had not wanted to see you so much. She says there is an old wound she has to heal."

Ivy Morris's hand stole toward her heart. "So many years," she murmured. "And what about the succession? Is that settled? Do they know who will take her place?"

"I'm not sure. Just a little while ago, when we were fighting with Beloved — "

Her grandmother's eyes widened. "What are you talking about? What has happened?"

Cara sighed. "I have a million things to tell you. But we've got to get back."

"Ah, a jailbreak! Well, I'm all for that. Do you have any ideas?"

CHAPTER TWENTY-FOUR

FLICKERFOOT

Cara felt a twinge of uncertainty. "I was hoping the ring would carry us back."

Her grandmother smiled. "Maybe it will. I suppose the best thing we can do is try."

Joining hands, they began to sing. But though they went twice through "Song of the Wanderer," the ring remained lifeless and dark.

Cara felt a new twist of fear. Had she come so far to find her grandmother only to end up trapped herself?

Then, on its own, the ring began to glow again.

A moment later they saw a form running toward them out of the green distance.

Cara cried out in joy.

It was Arabella Skydancer, Queen of the Unicorns.

Suddenly Cara felt fear begin to tangle with her joy.

The Queen looked free and strong in a way she had not seen her before, and though it was beautiful to see, she wasn't sure what it meant.

"I heard you," said the Queen when she reached them. "I heard you singing, your two voices calling me with your need."

"We hoped the song would take us back to our bodies," said Cara. "I had no idea it would call you to us." She reached toward the Queen, then drew her hand back. "Are you . . . are you all right?"

"That is hard to say. My body is nearly used up. But that makes it all the easier for me to run free of it when I need to — makes it all the easier to enter the light that flows between the worlds." She turned toward Cara's grandmother. The two gazed at each other for a long time without speaking.

It was the Queen who finally broke the silence. "Greetings, Wanderer. It has been a long time."

"Too long," said Ivy Morris softly, joy and sorrow mingling in her voice. She gestured to Cara. "I see you have met my granddaughter."

"She is a fine young woman. But then, that is no surprise."

Cara's pleasure at the compliment gave way to her

sense of urgency. "What did you mean about 'the light that flows between the worlds'? Where are we? What is this place?"

The Queen glanced around, as if assuring herself that she was where she had expected to be, then said, "Earth and Luster — and other worlds, as well, I suppose — are connected by light. In some places that light is splintered, broken into shafts, just as a rainbow is. Such places can be reached only by deep magic, and those who have mastered that magic sometimes use it as a means to exile their enemies. That is where we are now, in a place between the worlds, a place that is neither here nor there, not in one world or the other, but reflects bits and pieces of both of them. Taken together, these places are sometimes called the Rainbow Prison." She smiled. "Obviously, at the moment we are in the green shaft."

"Is there a red shaft, too?" asked Cara eagerly.

"Of course," said the Queen.

"I think my mother is there!"

"What do you mean?" asked the Wanderer.

Quickly, Cara told them of her experience with Grimwold's gem.

"It sounds, indeed, as if your mother is also somewhere in the Rainbow Prison," said the Queen. "Whether we can reach her is another matter altogether. Our first task is to get you and your grandmother out of *this* part of the prison."

"Can you do that?" asked Cara eagerly.

The Queen's face grew troubled. "I'm not sure. If your bodies were near my own, I could take you back with little problem. But I don't know where they are resting."

"They are still on Earth," said the Wanderer.

The Queen frowned. "This is worse than I feared."

Despite hours of trying, the Queen was not able to free them. Nor was she willing to leave them.

So they stayed together — the Old One, the Wanderer, and the girl who had traveled so far to reunite them — in the green shaft of the Rainbow Prison.

And, as the world shimmered around them, they talked.

Cara spoke first, telling the other two all of what had happened back on Earth.

The Old One and the Wanderer listened in silence until she described the way Beloved had fled after the fight in the living room.

"I do not like the sound of that," said the Queen. "Beloved does not give up so easily. I fear some deeper mischief is at work here."

Cara nodded. "I wondered about that, too. Only I couldn't figure out what. Beloved said something else that puzzled me — she said Lightfoot was next in line for the throne. Can that be true?"

The Queen sighed. "No. On that matter, Beloved is wrong. Lightfoot is not the heir to the throne."

"Then who is?" asked Ivy Morris, sounding startled.

The Queen looked away for a moment. When she looked back, her eyes were deep and strange and far-away looking. "I need to tell you a story. It is not one I am particularly eager to tell, for it does me little credit. But it is time it was known. It involves a young unicorn named Flickerfoot — possibly the most obstreperous, wayward, restless filly it has ever been my delight and exasperation to meet."

She sounds like fun, thought Cara.

"Flickerfoot was well named, for she was a Wanderer

at heart, and those feet took her far afield, carrying her into more danger and adventure than I care to tell you, or need to for this story. She was a source of great despair to her family — especially to her grandmother."

"Why her grandmother?" asked Cara, glancing sideways at her own grandmother.

"Because her grandmother had certain hopes and dreams for her, dreams that were endangered by Flickerfoot's wandering. I know this, because *I* was Flickerfoot's grandmother, and I tell you I loved her, as I had no other of my children, or my children's children — loved her in spite of her obstinate nature, or perhaps because of it. Loved her, and feared for her. Because Flickerfoot developed a passionate interest in the last place that I wanted her to wander."

"Earth," said Ivy Morris with quiet certainty.

"Earth," confirmed the Queen. "Our ancient home, which we love and fear, long for and mourn. By cajoling, spying, sneaking, exploring, and a dozen other means, Flickerfoot found the location of five of the seven gates that I have allowed to remain open. Despite my warning, my pleas, my threats, she began to travel back and forth between the two worlds. It was a forbidden trip — forbidden to all of us, and doubly forbidden to her because she was of the royal family. But she would not be restrained.

"Now, because of a promise made long ago by my own grandmother to a girl named Alma Leonetti, there is always one unicorn on Earth, one who remains to keep alive the memory of what we were, and what was lost when we left. That one, whom we call 'the Guardian of Memory,' is always in danger from Beloved and her children. Flickerfoot, whenever she crossed to Earth, shared that danger. Worse, she increased the danger by drawing more attention to our existence. But she insisted on going, and nothing I could do would stop her.

"Worse of all, she became attached — deeply attached — to a young tumbler named Jacques."

At these words both Cara and her grandmother drew in their breath.

"Finally I ordered Flickerfoot not to return to Earth anymore. It did no good. She was obsessed, and would return, despite any orders I might make.

"I lived in terror that she would be caught by Beloved and her Hunters, and finally hit on a plan to try to give her a measure of safety. I summoned the Geomancer and asked her if she could create for me a talisman that would carry a certain enchantment. M'Gama was uneasy with the idea, but agreed that it could be done — though it would certainly not be easy.

"I ordered her to do it.

"A year later — the most nerve-racking year of a very long life — the Geomancer returned with the item I had requested.

"I called Flickerfoot to me, and we affixed the talisman to her hoof. 'This is for use in only the most dire of emergencies,' I told her. 'But if the worst should happen, then strike your foot against stone as hard as you can and call on Earth itself to save you.' Then M'Gama gave her the specific words to activate the magic.

"Flickerfoot was wary of the talisman, and rightly so, but accepted it to calm my fears — or perhaps simply to silence me.

"For a year, all was well. Then — I know this because Jacques told me later — there came a day when Flickerfoot was visiting him on Earth and the Hunters found her trail. They began to pursue her. Flickerfoot and Jacques fled, but he soon realized that he was slow-ing her down, and so they separated. He was hoping to draw the pursuit in his direction. In this he failed, and the Hunters continued to trail her.

"That was the last time Jacques saw her — and the last I heard of my willful and beloved granddaughter for many years. But I was certain she had used M'Gama's talisman to save herself."

"How did you know?" asked Cara.

"Because I would have sensed it if she had been killed." The Queen shook her head in something like a shudder. "We all know, always and at once, when one of our kind is killed."

"But what did the talisman do?" persisted Cara.

The Queen hesitated. Her answer, when it came, was quiet, and laced with pain. "It transformed her into a human."

Ivy Morris cried out.

"It made her human," continued the Queen relentlessly, "and in so doing, saved her from the wrath of the Hunters — for how could they capture a unicorn where there was none? But the transformation had its price, as does all magic. When Flickerfoot lost her form, she lost, too, all memory of her past. Moreover, though she was several decades old, the magic translated those years into the much shorter life span of a human, leaving her but a girl."

"What happened next?" asked Cara eagerly.

"Much of what followed is a mystery. Where that girl went, lost and without memory, I do not know — though we do know, now, where she finally ended up. As for Jacques, my granddaughter had given him enough clues that he finally made his way to the gate she had been using to visit him." Arabella Skydancer sighed and shook her head. "It might have been better for all of us if I had simply closed those gates long ago. Anyway, Jacques found me and, in great despair, told me what little he knew. I assured him that though I did not know Flickerfoot's present location, she had indeed survived the Hunt. Then I invited him to remain in Luster, for I feared Earth was no longer safe for him, that Beloved and her children might now be seeking him as well. And, to be truthful, I also hoped his presence might somehow draw Flickerfoot back.

"Jacques did not accept my offer at first, for he insisted on returning to Earth to look for Flickerfoot. He was not the only one seeking her. The unicorns do have friends on Earth, and I set them all to seek my grand-daughter. But it was her brother who finally found her."

"Her brother?" asked Ivy, her voice strained, intense.

"Moonheart," said the Queen. Now she turned her face full on Ivy and said, "Though I never told him, and though he does not know to this day who you truly are, my Wanderer, the answer to his often asked question, 'Why was I able to sense Ivy's need all the way from her world to ours, when none of the others could?', is simple. You are his sister, my darling grand-daughter Flickerfoot."

Ivy Morris was weeping now, though whether the tears were of joy or sorrow, Cara could not tell. The Queen, too, was shedding tears.

"Why didn't you ever tell me this?" asked the Wanderer.

"For a long time I didn't know myself. When you arrived in Luster I took you for just another human who had stumbled through our gates — though from the first I felt my heart reaching out to you in a way it never had to any other human. It was M'Gama who finally worked it all out. But it took her years, and it was only shortly before you and Jacques had decided to marry that she deciphered the puzzle."

"That was why you tried to stop the wedding!" said Ivy with sudden understanding.

The Queen bowed her head in acknowledgment. "I have always regretted the bitter words that passed between us at that time, granddaughter, and wished that I could have dealt with the situation with more wisdom and grace. But even a queen, and a very old one at that, can bungle situations of the heart far too easily.

"Part of the problem was that by that time, you had lived so long as a human I did not know how you would react to the truth — especially since there was nothing I could do to return you to your form at that time."

"At that time?" asked Cara. "Does that mean you can turn her back now?"

"It means it is *possible* now. The spell was an act of desperation, and as such had desperate consequences, one of which was that there was no reversing it for fifty years. Now those years have passed. Even so, the task will not be easy. But it is time to begin. At last, it is time to begin. For the Wanderer is weary, as she well has a right to be, and her own true shape will bring her renewed strength and joy. Though she is old in human years, she is young as a unicorn, and will have that youth restored if we can make the transformation. And she is the rightful heir to the throne — which will be an enormous relief to poor Lightfoot."

Suddenly Cara caught her breath. Looking at the Queen and at her grandmother, she asked in a fearful whisper, "If Gramma is really a unicorn . . . *what am I?*"

The Queen smiled. "You are, like your mother, one of the strangest children ever born on two worlds. But more than that, you are, I hope, the one born to bring an end to the Hunt. Within your soul is merged not merely human and unicorn, but unicorn and Hunter. It all comes together in you, child."

Before Cara could answer, M'Gama's ring began to glow again.

CHAPTER TWENTY-FIVE

THE JOURNEY HOME

A voice came drifting through the green:

Oh, where's the thread that binds me,
The voice that calls me back?

"It's Jacques!" cried Cara. "He's singing us home!"

"How would he know to do that?" asked her grandmother, who looked distinctly nervous.

"Maybe he doesn't know. Maybe he's just doing the same thing I did — singing it to you, to your body, because . . . well, because it just seemed like the right thing to do. Come on — we have to sing with him if we're going to get back to our bodies."

Cara raised her voice to join the song. As she did, the green strand appeared again, stretching from

M'Gama's ring into the distance, back toward the song that Jacques was singing for them.

"Go," said the Queen urgently. "Don't lose this chance to escape, for you may not get another. I can get back to Luster on my own. Your amulet will bring you to me when you're ready, Flickerfoot. Come as soon as you can. Please."

Cara slipped her arm around her grandmother's waist. "Sing, Gramma," she pleaded. "I think we both have to be singing to make it work."

Indeed, the strand of green was clear but not solid, and Cara could not close her hand over it.

Reluctantly at first, then with increased strength and clarity, Ivy Morris joined the song.

Cara began to pull them along the green strand.

"I'll be waiting for you!" called the Queen. Then she turned and galloped in the opposite direction. Leaping into the swirling green, she disappeared from sight.

Cara felt the strand of green grow wispy beneath her hand. "Don't stop now, Jacques!" she cried. "Keep singing until we're home!"

"Jacques, you old fool, keep singing!" shouted Ivy. Then she took up the song again herself.

Whether he heard them, or it was mere luck, Jacques began to sing again. Cara and Ivy faltered for a moment, trying to match their voices to his. Then they began to move, slowly at first, then faster, and faster, until the greens blurred into a single color.

Cara gasped and opened her eyes. She was in her own body, back on Earth, back in her grandmother's bedroom. On the bed in front of her, the body of her grandmother, which had been so still and lifeless, was stirring too.

"You're back!" cried Jacques. The words tore from him like a sob. "*You're back!*"

Ivy Morris reached a hand toward him. "This is the last place I would have expected to see you, old friend."

"You're not the only one who can wander," he said, trying to force the corners of his drooping mouth into a smile.

"I wandered a little too far for comfort that time," said Ivy Morris. She drew in a deep breath. "Well. Rescued by my granddaughter and my former husband." She stopped, and her face twisted in a way that was unreadable. "And coming home with a story that suddenly makes sense of my life and also changes it utterly."

"What do you mean?" asked Jacques.

"Later," said Ivy Morris, her voice vague and troubled. "I'll explain everything later. Right now, based on the things Cara has told me, we have to move fast."

"Faster than she realizes," said Jacques.

Dread and fear were so heavy in his voice that it frightened Cara. "What do you mean?" she cried.

Jacques wrung his hands and looked away without speaking. Though his face was always lined and careworn, Cara had come to see that at least part of that was a mask, a pose. Now his features carried a look of pain that pierced her heart. She felt cold, wondering what new sorrow was in store.

"I should have stayed in Luster," he said dismally.

Cara put her hand on his arm. "You saved me! If you hadn't come through, Beloved would have had me."

He shook his head. "Thomas could have done that. It was his amulet that brought me through."

"Thomas has an amulet?" cried Cara in surprise.

Jacques nodded. "He let me take it so Lightfoot and

I could come after you. He wanted to come himself, but the amulet would only bring two of us, and I insisted that it be me, because . . . because I was hoping to find Ivy."

He turned his head away, and a racking sob tore from him.

"What's wrong?" asked Cara in alarm.

"The Hunters took it from me," moaned Jacques. "They took Thomas's amulet!"

She cried out, stunned by the horror of his words. Now she understood what Marcus must have been whispering just before the end, and why Beloved had made such a sudden retreat. Of course she had wanted to get away. She had what she was after. She had an amulet.

Cara's mind reeled at the thought of Beloved having a key to enter Luster.

Ivy Morris sprang to her feet. "We have to get this information to the Queen at once. Cara, may I have my . . . *our* amulet?"

Cara lifted the amulet from her neck and passed it to her grandmother. "What are you going to do?" she asked.

"Return to Luster. But only for a moment. I'll come back for you."

Closing her eyes at the same moment she closed her fingers over the crystal lid of the amulet, Ivy Morris whispered, "Luster, bring me home." In the words Cara heard a longing deeper than she would have imagined possible.

A moment later her grandmother was gone. The disappearance was silent, mysterious. She watched it but somehow could not see it. One moment her grandmother was there. Then Cara felt as if her vision had blurred, and when she looked again, her grandmother was gone.

Cara looked at Jacques. "Where will she end up?" she asked nervously.

"With the Queen," said Jacques, and Cara suddenly remembered what Grimwold had told them: that for her grandmother, the amulet was a direct route not only to Luster, but to the Queen herself.

She took Jacques' hand, wondering what, if anything, she should say to him of the things she had learned in the Rainbow Prison. But before she could speak, her grandmother reappeared at the edge of the bed. "Message delivered," she said grimly.

"Is the Queen angry?" asked Jacques, his voice trembling.

"'Angry' is not the word," said Ivy. She stretched out her hand to him. "This is not a good way for either of us to meet again, old friend. We will talk later, and if you have half as much to tell me as I have to tell you, it will be a long conversation indeed. For now, be at ease. The Queen sends her forgiveness, and bids you remember that had you not come through to Earth, you would not have been here to call Cara and me back from the Rainbow Prison, something it is unlikely Thomas would have done. I owe you my life, dear fool, and not for the first time. But we must move now, and move fast, before the transit point shifts."

"What are we going to do?" asked Cara.

Her grandmother smiled. "Set up a relay system. Right now, and for a little while longer, the amulet will take *you* back to Ebillan's cave. I want you to return there and, one by one, bring back your friends — at least those who wish to go to Autumngrove with us."

"Autumngrove?" asked Cara, feeling confused. "What about Summerhaven?"

"Summer is ending," said her grandmother. "The

311

court is already on the move. Now, come along; let's check on the others."

Ian Hunter was lying where Cara had left him. But he was awake now, and when his daughter, Jacques, and the Wanderer came down the stairs and entered the living room, he cried out in astonishment. He sprang to his feet, then staggered and sank to the couch again. Despite Lightfoot's healing work, he was still weak from the wound Beloved had inflicted on him.

His cry roused Lightfoot, who pushed himself to his feet more slowly. "Welcome, Wanderer," he said, bowing his horn to Ivy Morris. "We have traveled a long way to find you."

"Indeed you have," said Ivy Morris. "I understand you have been a good friend to my granddaughter. For that, you have my thanks, and the thanks of the Queen as well."

Ian Hunter stood again, more slowly now, and took a step toward them. His face was unreadable.

Ivy Morris reached out to him. "We have much to speak of," she whispered. "And much that needs to be forgiven on both sides. But Cara has told me what happened in this room last night, and if you are willing to set aside the past, then I am as well."

Cara stared at her family, or what there was of it here, confused by the tangle of joy and sorrow that bound her to the grandmother who was so much more than she seemed; to the father whom she had lost and found and lost and found yet again; and to the man who might be her grandfather.

But the time for talking, for understanding, for healing, would have to come later. Now she had to travel again.

Taking the amulet from her grandmother, Cara asked Luster to bring her home.

She returned to the crystal cave from which she had left. Moving quickly, but cautiously, she followed the dark tunnel that led to the larger cave that Ebillan called home.

She found them, her "family of the road," waiting at the front of the cave. The Squijum was the first to notice her. "Girl back!" he cried, bounding to her side and scrambling up to her shoulder. "Girl back!"

Ebillan turned his massive head in her direction.

"So, the little Wanderer returns, having slipped away while I was distracted."

"I apologize for my ungracious departure," she said, speaking in the courtly language of the dragons.

"No matter. Your friend was as good as his word, and for the mending he did of my wedding cup, I am willing to forgive perhaps more than I should. I notice, however, that you are alone. What of the friends who followed you to Earth?"

"Safe, and waiting for us to join them," said Cara.

Then, speaking quickly and telling only a fraction of what had happened since she'd left the cave, she explained the plan for returning to the Queen's court.

"Perhaps I should install a tollgate," said Ebillan testily.

"What's to complain about?" snapped Moonheart. "You'll be rid of us all sooner than you expected. I should think you would be relieved."

Ebillan grumbled his annoyance, but said no more.

"Earth?" growled the Dimblethum uneasily. "Then to court? The Dimblethum does not like this idea."

"It's either that or walk back the long way, you drad-blatted fool," said Medafil, stretching his wings behind him. "As for me, I plan to fly, and not to any court. It's time I headed for home."

Cara hurried to the gryphon's side. "I shall miss you," she said, stroking the feathers on his neck.

"Gaah! I'll miss you, too. But I notice you didn't bring the Wanderer back with you. Never will get that gutbumbled kiss, I suppose."

"Here's one from me until you see her," said Cara, stretching up to kiss his yellow beak.

"Gaah!" he said. But from lower in his body came a deep rumble. It took Cara a second to realize he was purring.

"We don't have time for long good-byes," said Moonheart. "The day will be over soon. If we're going to make this crossing, we need to start *now*."

Cara glanced out of the cave. The sun was appallingly close to the horizon. She turned to Ebillan. "With your permission, we will depart," she said, speaking once more in the guttural, fiery language of dragons.

"Permission granted — on the condition you do not return to my cave. Our dealings with each other are at an end."

"Terms accepted," said Cara.

She gave Medafil a final hug, then led her friends to the crystal cave where, one by one, she ferried them through to Earth.

The Dimblethum hung back with the clear intent of being the last to go. But when she came back for him, he shook his head sadly and said, "The Dimblethum will miss Cara. The Dimblethum will miss Lightfoot. But the Dimblethum will not go to court."

Cara felt her heart clench with sorrow. "Where will you go instead?"

"The Dimblethum goes to his own home, back to where you first met him."

"But how will you get across the wasteland?" she cried. "I can't stand to think of you crossing that all alone."

"I'm going to fly the fitbingled creature," said Medafil crossly. "don't know why. Stupid idea. But I offered, and there it is. Probably break my back. I'll guide him through the forest, too."

Cara laughed, despite the tears that were rolling down her cheeks. Then she flung herself against the Dimblethum and held him as tightly as she could.

"Go," he said at last, pushing her away from him. "Go now, while you can."

She looked up. The sun was almost gone.

She raced to the crystal cave, and let the amulet carry her back to Earth.

CHAPTER TWENTY-SIX

THE BROKEN HORN

With five humans, four unicorns, and the Squijum inside it, the living room of the little house Cara had shared with her grandmother was more crowded than she had ever seen it.

What made it feel even more crowded was the tension that crackled from the unicorns' barely-contained anger at finding themselves sharing the space with a Hunter.

The sharing was not going to last long because soon they would be leaving for Luster.

Ian Hunter took his daughter aside to talk with her. They sat in the kitchen, looking at each other across the shabby little table where she used to sit to eat her breakfast. Neither spoke for several minutes.

It was her father who finally broke the silence. "You are a miracle," he said.

"I'm a wanderer," whispered Cara.

"And the most precious thing in the world to me," he answered, reaching out to take her hand. She slipped her hands forward. He folded them into his own, which were callused and hard with muscle. "We have to make a decision now," he said at last.

Though he did not speak it aloud, they both knew what that decision was.

Cara sat staring at him, at the lean, dark-eyed face, nearly haggard now, the face that had hunted her and haunted her and that meant so much to her heart. Stared at it, and with pain choking her throat finally whispered, "I have to go back to Luster."

He closed his eyes and nodded in acceptance. "You do understand that I cannot go with you."

"Why not? I bet the Queen would forgive you. I bet it would be —"

He shook his head. "I have to find your mother first."

Warm relief flooded her heart. "How will you do it?"

He looked away for a moment. "I am a Hunter," he

said at last. Then he turned back. "I must stay for another reason, Cara. The danger to Luster is growing now that Beloved has an amulet. I will do what I can to discover her plans, to help warn the unicorns of when and where the attack will come, as come it must. It won't be easy; I'm marked as a traitor now to the Hunters, and it is unlikely any unicorn will trust me either. But I may be able to help somehow."

"Every time I find you, I lose you again," said Cara, trying not to let her sorrow overwhelm her.

"I could say the same thing," he replied gently. "But it's different this time, Cara. Long ago you were taken from me, and I still carry a wound from that loss that no unicorn can heal. When we met in Firethroat's cave, I lost you in a different way." He smiled. "Your friend the dragon dropped me about as far from civilization as was possible. On the journey back I had a great deal of time to think — and what I thought about most was how amazing you are. And how the things that had been drilled into me by Beloved and the Hunters, the things I believed utterly, no longer seemed quite so certain."

He shook his head. "And now we part again, but not

in the same way. Because this time each of us knows the other's heart — knows that as soon as it can be managed, we'll be together again."

She slipped from her chair, went to him, and put her arms around his neck. When she pulled away again, her cheeks were wet with his tears.

Autumngrove was even more beautiful than Summerhaven, but the beauty was little balm for the sorrow that enfolded the unicorns.

The Queen was fading, and would not last much longer.

A glory was gathering, unicorns streaming into Autumngrove from all directions to bid farewell to their queen — and not only unicorns. Those humans who had gotten the word were traveling to pay their respects, too — as were many of the other creatures of Luster.

The gathering had started two weeks earlier, when the court was still in Summerhaven and concern about the Queen had reached the point that the unicorns put out a call for the farewells to begin. There had been a great deal of discussion about whether the Queen should make the trip to Autumngrove. She was the one who had insisted on going, and had succeeded in forcing the others to accept her decision.

Behind the sorrow was enormous concern, for the matter of who would take the Queen's place was still uncertain. Though the rules of succession had left Lightfoot in line for the throne, it was well known that he did not want the position.

And strange rumors had begun to circulate that there was someone else — someone unexpected — who might take the Queen's place. Other rumors were spreading, too — rumors of a growing danger from Beloved, and the possibility of a fierce, final battle that would decide the ancient struggle between the unicorns and the Hunters once and for all.

This was the state of things two days after Cara returned to Luster, and it was causing Lightfoot terrible anxiety. "I thought she would live forever," he said miserably to Cara as they walked in the woods of Autumngrove one afternoon. "I can't do this. I don't want to do this!"

"I don't want you to have to," she said sympathetically.

"You're nicer about it than my uncle. When I said this to him, he told me to stop whining. Then he went on about how when the Queen was well my shirking of responsibility was merely annoying, but now that she is going to leave us, it becomes" — and here he lowered his voice to imitate Moonheart — "'something deeper — something we cannot afford.' As if this was simply some chore I didn't want to take on."

"Why don't you want to do it?" asked Cara.

"Because I'm wrong for it! I'd make a mess of it! I can't believe they even want me to try. Any fool can see I'd be horrible at it."

"So why do they want you to? I could never quite figure out how it works here."

"Oh, it's nothing as simple as it is on Earth where the King's firstborn son follows him onto the throne and everyone else can just go off and play."

"Actually, it does sometimes get more complicated than that," said Cara gently.

"Well, at least there are some sort of predetermined rules. Here we have a ceremony where a group of unicorns read signs from the water, the sky, and the forest. You wouldn't believe how surprised everyone was when they announced that I was next in line for the throne.

They were as upset about it as I was. The only difference was, they kept saying, 'You have to accept your destiny,' and *I* kept saying, 'There's been some sort of horrible mistake!'"

He paused, then added more calmly, "To tell you the truth, I think there are times when Moonheart believes we should just ignore the signs; after all, they were less clear than they should have been. We both know that he would make a better king than I would. But when I tell him that, he gets more upset than ever. And to make things worse, now we're facing the possibility of an invasion by the Hunters. And who knows what the delvers might be getting up to. The last thing we need at the moment is me as the King!"

He shook his head and sighed. "Given how hard I worked to get away from the court, the fact that I ended up back here at this time is almost enough to make me believe that the Greater Powers really do want me to be the King — which, in my opinion, would mean that Moonheart is wrong. *I'm* not the silliest and most irresponsible thing in the kingdom. They are!"

◆　◆　◆

M'Gama arrived in Autumngrove two days after Cara and her group had returned, announcing that she had come to observe the passing of the Queen. Cara sought her out and told her all that had happened since they had last been together.

"I'm glad the ring was of use," said M'Gama.

Cara and her grandmother shared a grove much like the one Cara had been given at Summerhaven — a private place surrounded by a thick wall of shrubbery that was turning silvery with the autumn. But despite sharing this sleeping space, Cara did not see much of her grandmother, for Ivy Morris spent most of her time with the Queen.

When they did have time together, the two of them talked long and deeply.

But what neither of them brought up was the startling story that the Queen had told them while they were in the Rainbow Prison. It seemed to be fearful territory somehow, and Ivy was either unwilling or unable to discuss it.

One night they were called to the Queen's grove, a beautiful spot beside a silvery stream. Many unicorns were gathered there already. Their horns were dim, their heads hung low.

The Queen lay at the edge of the swiftly flowing water, so weary she could not lift her head.

Cara felt hot grief overwhelm her, and struggled to keep from disturbing the sacred moment with a wail of despair.

She saw a handful of humans scattered about the grove; Jacques and Thomas were there, as was — to her surprise — Armando. She saw others as well, humans she did not recognize, including a cloaked woman who gave an impression of great age.

The unicorns began to sing, a song that seemed to be made as much of light as of sound.

One by one the unicorns approached their Queen, knelt, nuzzled her neck, or laid their horns across her shoulder. Cara knew they were speaking to her in private, mind to mind, a last exchange of words and wishes, blessings and sorrows.

Occasionally the Queen would raise her head or nicker softly. Mostly she lay without moving.

One of the unicorns — her face so mournful, it took Cara a moment to recognize her as Laughing Stream — came to her and said, "It is your turn now."

Swallowing hard, Cara went to the Queen. Kneeling, she placed her hand gently on the frail, white curve of her neck.

"Greetings, Great-great-granddaughter," thought the Queen. "I must apologize for leaving so soon after you have come to stay with us. I owe you many thanks, for you have given me my heart's desire — you returned my wandering granddaughter."

"My heart has a desire, too," thought Cara, "and that is for you to stay with us."

"Don't be cruel," replied the Queen gently. "My time has come, and I must move on. I welcome it, for I am more weary than you can imagine. I have given instructions that you are to be allowed to drink from the Queen's pool. Think carefully before you accept this boon. It will add many years to your life, which can be a blessing, or a burden, depending on how you spend them."

"What about . . . about Flickerfoot?"

"Keep watching," replied the Queen, and Cara actually sensed a note of amusement in the thought. "With luck, all will be resolved. Now you must leave me, for there are others I need to speak to, and my time is short. I wish I had had more time to know you."

"And I you, Great-great-grandmother," whispered Cara with her mind and her lips.

When she lifted her hand from the Queen's neck her fingers tingled, as if she had been holding light and it had soaked into them.

Other humans were summoned to approach the Queen. Each knelt, and Cara saw that while they were with her their faces were transformed by a look of bliss, but that when they stood to leave, grief overwrote it and tears spilled down their cheeks.

Ivy Morris was last to be called. She knelt by the Queen, then fell forward across her neck, weeping with despair. This impropriety brought a gasp from the assembled unicorns — a gasp quickly replaced by a cry of mingled sorrow and joy as the Queen, the Old One, vanished.

Thomas, who had come to stand behind Cara, tightened his hands on her shoulders, and she wondered if he saw what she had seen: the Queen rise from the ground, looking as young and as strong as when she had been in the Rainbow Prison, though no more substantial than a beam of light. She had stood, staring down at the Wanderer for a moment, then turned to

look around the circle of loved ones, bowing and smiling to each of them. Then she stepped onto the stream and, laughing herself, let the laughing water carry her away.

Now there was nothing left of her body except the horn, which lay glowing in pearly perfection beneath the stricken form of the Wanderer.

M'Gama stepped forward and slid the horn from beneath Ivy Morris's body. Holding it in both hands, she raised it above her head. Deep silence filled the clearing, as if the stream itself were holding its breath.

"What I do now, I do at the Queen's bidding," said M'Gama, her voice low but powerful. "The Queen's council knows this to be true."

She turned in a slow circle so that all could see the horn. Then, with one swift movement, she raised her knee, brought the horn down sharply against it, and snapped it in half. The unicorns cried out in horror, then fell silent as a rush of wind swept through the clearing, clean, clear, and ripe with magic. The leaves swirled up in dancing patterns, and silver stars seemed to rain about them. Cara thought, for just a moment, that she heard the Queen herself, singing.

And then Ivy Morris stood, and cried out in joy and in pain as she shed the false form that had imprisoned her for so many decades, and returned at last to her own true shape and name.

"Behold!" cried M'Gama, pointing to the beautiful young unicorn. "I give you Amalia Flickerfoot, long-lost granddaughter of Arabella Skydancer, returned at last from wandering and exile in time to bid her grandmother farewell. Amalia Flickerfoot, rightful Queen of the unicorns!"

A cry, a song, a shout rose from the clearing.

The queen is gone. Long live the queen!

And that is the story of how the one who was lost was found, of how one who wandered at last made her way back home.

What happened next, how Beloved made her attempt on Luster, and the battle that followed, is another story altogether.

It is recorded, like all such tales, in the Unicorn Chronicles.